What Part of the Game is Dat?

ANGELO BARNES

Order this book online at www.trafford.com
or email orders@trafford.com

Most Trafford titles are also available at major online book retailers.

Print information available on the last page.

ISBN: 978-1-6987-1629-9 (sc)
ISBN: 978-1-6987-1630-5 (e)

Library of Congress Control Number: 2024900783

Trafford rev. 01/11/2024

 www.trafford.com
North America & international
toll-free: 844-688-6899 (USA & Canada)
fax: 812 355 4082

Contents

PRAISE BE TO ALLAH

WE DID IT

What Part Of The Game Is Dat?

Picture taking a charge for a childhood friend who left you high and dry. That's what happened to a young shooter and hustler from the old Flag House Projects in East Baltimore. After Bradshaw did seven hard years, learning from past mistakes made him a better man, one determined to never go back to prison. With intentions to stay away from the game, he is released to the same people, places and things.

Crossed by his son's mother, dragged on by a homeboy, and alienated by immediate family endangered his transition. In the mist of the drama, he is loved by a pupil on the come up. Will loyalty or a concealed thirst for revenge block Bradshaw from unforeseen opportunities? Time will tell.

From the author who brought you *666 Pimpin* and *Suicide Bible: The story of Natosha Little*, open your mind to this Flag House saga. Take a stroll into that project life where fact and fiction draws a thin line.

What Part of the Game is Dat?

A NOVEL BY: ANGELO BARNES

BOOK ONE

CHAPTER 1

This morning Bradshaw's eyes opened to the same collage of photos that's been staring at him for the past seven years. Most of the images on the wall were of his son's mother, few of Doobie. He often refrained from referring to Peaches by name because it evoked so many mixed emotions. As with the rest of his close friends and relatives who abandoned him during his incarceration, reserving Irvin as an exception, a lonely pillow was the reminder of how Peaches recently jumped ship. He suffered through a full calendar without contact from her nor Doobie. A ten year sentence was steep for drugs found in a car, especially when his bunky was a serial bank robber serving only twenty beans. A Possession with Intent to Distribute wasn't worth ripping a man from his loved ones. Denied by the Board two autumns ago, Bradshaw made note to mention that exact thought in his parole hearing scheduled for noon.

Prison froze his youth at twenty-three, which was his original age when sentenced. Bradshaw's ebony tone remained smooth and even, owing to daily exercise, water and a lot of rest. His disingenuous features made the average person desire to address him by any name besides the one on his identification card. Small lips and a large nose gave him the appearance of a Lamont, Jermaine or Deon. When adding bug eyes, thick brows, an egg-shaped head and rangy physique to the equation, he looked more like a Joe, Charles or Frank. With an even cut or a cap, suit or jeans, regardless of the presentation, his face always rang familiar.

As Bradshaw rose to care for his hygiene, he glanced at his celly on the top bunk playing possum. "You ain't snoring, so I know you woke."

Vic stretched and yawned like a vampire preparing for coffin time. He spoke groggily, "I tossed and turned through the night like you. Farts kept me up."

"Sho' ya right," Bradshaw lathered his rag at the sink.

"Big day, huh?" Vic popped a peppermint in his mouth to combat morning breath.

Bradshaw gave a halfhearted smile, "Yeah, but I ain't looking for no rhythm from them people. When I caught this ten, I was looking to do nine years, eleven months and twenty-nine days."

A speck of disappointment settled within Vic. Being an elder, he schooled Bradshaw, "That's just your defenses on high alert. Ain't nothing in this rat hole but a bunch of dead men too stubborn to lie down. Real life is on the other side of that gate. Claim it, and let destiny work."

"Just don't want my hopes up to have them shot down, did that the first time." Bradshaw washed his face.

Vic knew nervousness was a natural reaction, so he endeavored to comfort his cellmate. "Never know what you ducked by being in here. Before now, you could'a been rushing out this door straight into a funeral home. Two years ago wasn't your time, might've not been ready. I'm sure this has been a tough journey, as with the rest of us who hate jail, but the sun might shine through ya' dark cloud. Ain't shit gonna go right if you don't walk into that room chest first, chin high, positive. Get it?"

"Got it." Bradshaw squeezed a glob of toothpaste on his toothbrush. "Easier said than done."

Noon came so fast Bradshaw almost ran late. Despising the insensitive nature of the parole process, Bradshaw sat in front of a cheerless three; the Commissioner, Boards spokesman, resembled Santa Clause. At the right of Santa was a chubby black woman who could have chosen a better wig. To his left was an institutional case manager, distinguished by an oval head, gray at the temples. They were an awkward bunch by any standard, each holding a third of his freedom in the palm of their hands.

The case manager gave a summary of Bradshaw's institutional record, "Mr. Peatican has a spotless adjustment history. He obtained his GED as well as certificates from several cognitive programs. Currently working as a tutor at the school, staff consider him a model inmate."

The woman cringed before forcing a smile. "Prison is a controlled environment where an inmate doesn't have all the temptations of the world which got him here in the first place. A guy can be at his best behind these walls. What counts is if you can do the same thing in society without fail. That's our focus."

Feeling the need to defend himself, Bradshaw showed humbleness while expressing his point, "The same drugs out there is in here, same violent mentality, the works. But what makes it more complicated is that I can't escape it by going into my house and closing the door. There's nowhere to run in this place. Doing time is no walk in the park, so a lot of these dudes depend on a high to help them cope, but I stayed away from all that negativity, used time wisely to make myself a better person. I put in hard work to reach this level of knowledge and patience. As crazy as it sounds, my sentence has been a blessing."

Santa Clause interjected, "I see model prisoners as criminals who' ve mastered a ruse to beat the system. If you're doing so well in jail, maybe this is where you need to stay."

4

"Don't get it twisted," Bradshaw cleaned up the man's misconception, completely forgetting the mental note he made to himself earlier, "I hate this concentration camp, and I'll never be able to reach my fullest potential in here without the proper resources. I'm not gonna lie, I haven't changed into a new person. I just learned how to better deal with the old me. The last image I left my son was negative, and I don't want him to make the same choices as I have. I'm beggin' for one opportunity to go out there and save my kid."

The woman examined some papers in a folder. His Statement of Facts was comprised of complicated angles. "It says that you were caught with a kilo of cocaine in your trunk."

"It wasn't mine."

"But you plead guilty to it," uttered Santa. "The reason why we denied you before was because you never took responsibility for your crime."

The mental note finally came but was discarded. Even though his own version of the story was true, Bradshaw swallowed his pride so fast it almost produced heartburn. He told them what they wanted to hear. "I apologize for my actions. I'm through with the streets and selling drugs. I paid for my mistake, and now I'm ready to fly straight."

Every eye bounced off the other as those within the room fell silent. Santa seldom smiled. When he did, some poor prisoner was about to catch his wrath. He said as his cheeks reddened, "You seem honest enough. For that reason, I'm recommending immediate parole."

Elated, Bradshaw put his hands together as he thanked them, "I won't let y'all down."

The woman concluded, "The only way to stay out of prison is to not break any law. You're thirty years young with a lot of life left to live. So, if you mishandle this opportunity, it won't be us you're letting down, it'll be yourself. You should receive an official decision in a few weeks. Good luck."

Bradshaw kissed more ass, shook hands and exited the room. Stunned by the outcome, he floated on cloud nine all the way back to the tier. Bradshaw conveyed the news to Vic soon as he stepped in the cell, embracing his bunky and giving dap.

"They recommended my release."

Vie jumped for joy as if he was leaving also. "I know dat's right. You're on your way, son. Just keep your good news low. You know these crab-in-a-barrel-ass negroes will get jealous and hate."

Contemplating the last hurdle, Bradshaw's gaze slowly met the floor. "It still has to get approved."

"Don't worry about it," Vic cracked open a box of debbies, "you're good as gone."

$ $ $ $

Despite Bradshaw's pessimism, parole was granted on May 11, 1997. After seven long years, anxiety was expected. He left all prison possessions to Vic. Dressed in state-issued garbs, Bradshaw parted Jessup Correctional Institution with fifty dollars from his reserve account. A cab charged him a standard forty bucks from Jessup to the Inner Harbor. During the ride, the Malian driver sparked up friendly conversation.

"Hey, buddy," he scanned his passenger through the rearview mirror, "how's it feel to be free?"

Speeding on the highway gave Bradshaw a queasy sensation. "Don't know yet."

"What's the first thing you plan on doing?" He doled a look that said *pussy, pussy, pussy.*

Bradshaw wished the driver kept his eyes on the road. "Gettin' my life back on track. Staying out of prison is my main objective."

"Sure, buddy." The Malian gestured his head in a way that implied he'd heard it all before.

Instead of being dropped off at the original destination, good conversation landed him on Ashland Avenue with no extra fee.

Warm weather birthed glossy blue clouds. Bradshaw beheld the beautiful sky as he approached Peaches' front door. He stood in the morning hour pondering the suspense. The many restless nights in a cell when he pictured this moment, adlibbing and reliving it a thousand times in the mind. Now everything but the result was made manifest. Only the next few minutes could determine if his past thoughts would play out to perfection. He knocked on the door with so much anticipation it was almost as though Peaches was the one who'd just been released. Bradshaw had to knock twice before the door opened.

A thug in boxers greeted him with a scowl. "Yo, I believe you got the wrong spot," he said.

Studying the bird-chested chump, Bradshaw could barely speak. With every fuse blown, his brain took a second to load. Common sense advised him not to leap to conclusions, but jumbled thoughts complicated his feelings. He took another glance at the door number, then uttered, "No, this is indeed the right house."

Wearing a confused stare that said more than words, the thug scratched at his own nuts.

A female's voice echoed from the background, "Who's dat, baby?"

Slim was bewildered. "I don't know...some nigga!"

Drunk with anger, Bradshaw's lips twitched. He balled up his fist, attempting to resist behaving in a violent manner. "Tell Peaches to come to this door."

Just then, before shit got crump, his son's mother emerged from a back room. Pink lingerie made her petite body prettier than ever before. The sight of Bradshaw left her breathless. Searching for an explanation, she exclaimed, "It's not what you think...I..."

Bradshaw cut her off, "Save it! Where the fuck is my son?"

As if the thug was the one who had to present an answer, he hunched his shoulders without a definitive reason.

Peaches shoved him into the house. "Doobie is in school."

If Bradshaw wasn't so worried about going back to prison, he would have gotten a real buzz out of physically punishing Peaches and her male friend. The luck was on them he'd taken up anger management while away. "So, this is the reason you stopped writing and coming to see me? Sold out our relationship for some dick. Hope you're happy." He shook his head and walked away.

The brown-skinned beauty followed him barefoot. "Baby, I'm sorry. I'll make him leave. He's not anyone special. I wanna be wit chu."

Bradshaw smacked her hands away with force. "Don't change on my account. Just tell Doobie Ill be back to see him. As far as you, I ain't fuckin' wit it. That's dead. Count me out."

Peaches covered her face and wept as he went about his business.

$ $ $ $

En route to the projects, Bradshaw tried to replace the thoughts of Peaches by tuning into the hood. He heard his stomp took a turn for the worst. Flag House was already bad before he got locked up, but now it was referred to as a war zone. Bradshaw knew all the pushers and was sure his name still rung bells around the way. He grew up in Flag House Projects, plus his family still lived there. As he was about to cut through Dunbar field, a red Lexus passed him and slammed on brakes. Deep tints prevented Bradshaw from seeing inside the car. When the driver-side door swung open, Irvin jumped out, all teeth.

Bradshaw was relieved.

Decked out in the latest fashion, sporting long braids that complimented his light complexion, Irvin joked, "I almost put dat hammer on you, boy."

Bradshaw honestly replied, "And you almost seen me take off on ya' dumb-ass. You ugly as shit."

The men sized up each other before dapping. Irvin was his little man he groomed in the projects. In fact, Irvin was the only one who kept it real by staying in touch and sending loot through the years.

But it just wasn't about the money; true friendship and loyalty was what kept the boy in his left tittie. Fate was a motherfucker. What were the odds of them running into one another by chance.

Irvin looked in his mentor's eyes with sincere admiration. "Why you ain't tell ah nigga you was gittin' out? Could'a scooped you up from the jail."

The truth was he knew the lifestyle Irvin was living and didn't want to jump straight out the cell into the arms of temptation. "I wanted it to be a surprise. Plus, with all my past dirt, I don't know which one of these cats might've been waiting in some bushes for me."

"Excuses." Irvin shooed him off. "Fuck them niggas. They ain't stupid."

"That don't mean sleep on the enemy. I taught you better than that."

With that priceless point going in and out his ears, Irvin took stock of Bradshaw's attire. "I got some time to burn. Where you was on ya' way too?"

"My mother's," answered Bradshaw.

"Put dat on hold 'cause I'm 'bout to take you shoppin'. I can't have my nigga lookin' like ah state baby."

Holding only ten dollars in his pocket, Bradshaw couldn't see himself turning down the offer. "Cool."

Irvin smiled. "Let's blast."

During their trip to the Towson Mall, Bradshaw caught up with current events. "What's up with that nigga Grub?"

Irvin replied with a frown, "Yo in power. He out this bitch runnin'num up.

Bradshaw and Grub used to be partners before he went in, but the fat fucker left him out to dry. He felt slighted only because the kilo Butcher found in the car belonged to Grub. Nevertheless, regardless of the circumstances, like a true gangster, Bradshaw didn't rat; he took the fall and did the time.

"So he the hog with the big nuts, huh?"

Irvin continued, "The nigga rich. He even own the barbershop down Flag, bought it with cash from that old couple who used to own it. But that's not the only property he got."

Bradshaw shifted into a troublesome question. "Where he banggin' at?"

"Mainly Flag. He got the hood on smash!"

That made him pissed though he responded with ease, "Can't knock the hustle."

"To me....," Irvin lit a smoke, "that nigga owes you big time. How you plan on making him pay up?"

Bradshaw spoke against what he really felt, "I made the choice to break law. He owes me nothing. I don't want anything to do with him. That's it."

"Success is the greatest revenge. When you get back to the papers —"

"I'm through with throwing bricks at the penitentiary. A regular job will suit me fine."

Not convinced, Irvin smirked. "Well, if you just so happen to change ya' mind, I got chu."

Bradshaw didn't respond.

The topic was switched. ""What's up wit Peaches?""

That question added more birch to Bradshaw's inner flame. "I was coming from there when you ran into me. I knocked, a nigga came to the door."

"Fuck no," muttered Irvin, feeling an urge to turn the car around.

Bradshaw had fire in his eyes. "Bitch had me thinking she wasn't out here fuckin'. Even when she stopped hollering at me, I figured she just needed a little break; any woman holding a dude down deserves one from time to time. If Peaches was straight up and told me she wanted to move on, I could've better dealt with the situation. But she lied. That's what crushed me the most."

Irvin felt his pain. "I know two birds out Cherry Hill that be on some freak shit. I can hit'um while we in'nah mall to see if they tryna link up. It's ya' call..."

Still trying to shake the thought of Peaches, Bradshaw obliged, "Bet."

$ $ $ $

Irvin spent five bands on Bradshaw without a wink. At the duration of their pricey shopping spree, the girls were contacted and placed on standby.

An hour later, whipping into Cherry Hill, a gang of hustlers and fiends treasured the Lexus as it pulled up to a rowhouse on Seamen Avenue. Irvin honked the horn, and two young ladies emerged, both fine as hell.

"Bitches bad, ain't they?"

Bradshaw bounced his chin in agreement, gawking at the approaching females. "Good taste."

Irvin frowned, bottom lip poked out. "Let cha boy work."

Once inside the car, without a shy spell, both women smiled cordially. Bradshaw deduced which was for him by the way they reacted to his little homie. One girl kissed Irvin before introducing herself as Candice. The other was caramel, short hair curled stylishly. As she settled into the back seat, her and Bradshaw magnetically locked eyes, passion building between the two. The connection was evident.

She was second to announce, "I'm Tina."

Distant from a talkative mood, Bradshaw nodded impassively.

Irvin broke the monotony, "We 'bout to hit the hotel."

Candice spoke her peace, "As long as you got a few dollars and some piff, it's whatever."

"You ain't said shit." Irvin showed a ball of cash and a sandwich bag of loud. He passed the grass over to Candice, and she started rolling.

Being on papers, not trying to catch a contact, Bradshaw cracked the window as they puffed.

The unfamiliar pair made themselves comfortable inside the room. He flicked through the channels while Tina sprawled herself across the bed.

She asked, "How long you knew Irvin?"

Taken by the girl's nosiness, he explained, "Forever...I practically raised him."

His answer was intriguing. "Then why I ain't seen you before?"

A stare for stare was exchanged.

"I was locked up seven years."

"When were you released?"

Bradshaw nonchalantly responded in a single word, "Today."

Tina lustfully pried, "Have you had some pussy?"

"Not yet."

She was pleased. "Lucky me."

$ \qquad $ \qquad $ \qquad $

The four were gone by check-out time the following day. Both girls got dropped off with messed-up hairdos, walking crooked. Irvin snickered as he shot Bradshaw to the parole spot. "How was the gutz."

Bradshaw paused, then sighed, "Amazin, completely different from Palma Court."

Irvin laughed. "You been beatn' your meat, livin' that jail life for too long. Out here is the real world where money rules. If a spiritual man came home broke, he'd starve and die sleepin' on ah cardboard box. You gotta treat yourself to make up for all the years you missed with your life on hold. Cash is freedom, pleasure is divine. In God we trust...and with that trust comes mad pussy, cars, clothes, nice homes and more."

Bradshaw's dull expression wasn't fit for the conversation. To agree would've been speaking too fast. Irvin reiterated the same point in several ways until Bradshaw exited the car.

About twenty to thirty paces later, navigating himself through a maze of fiends hanging out front the parole spot, he cleared a metal detector, leading him to a congested reception area inside. The room was bland with long pews, no windows. Broken promises and old prison stories were the scope of loud chatter. An hour in this woeful place seemed like a lifetime. Just before he got too bored, a moppy-haired white guy peeped out from a secured door, pointed to Bradshaw, and motioned for him to come forth.

"Are you Mr. Petican?" he asked, looking at a folder through thick glasses.

Bradshaw answered quickly, "The one and only."

"Follow me," he said without blinking.

The men shuffled through sharp turns of a front hallway, reaching a tiny office. One desk and two chairs literally ate up the entire space. It reminded Bradshaw of a cell, calling him into the realization of claustrophobia having many levels. Once seated, the parole officer got down to business.

"I'm Mr. Bart, and I'll be monitoring your transition with a fine- toothed comb. Let's first talk about your home address. 1208 Ashland Avenue, is that correct?"

Bradshaw wanted no more dealings with Peaches. "Naw, I need to switch that to my mother's address at 107 Lombard Street. The Apartment is 7H."

Never experiencing the dangerous area beyond a car's window, a portrait of the slummy projects froze in his mind. "Are you referring to Flag House Projects?"

"Yes sir."

The answer stung Mr. Bart, causing him to judge a book by its cover, He fingered through a file. "Do you have employment plans?"

Bradshaw's eyes rolled north. "I was thinking about going back to school, getting a trade, my CDL's, forklift certification, or—"

Mr. Bart shut him down. "Enthuse me with the short version."

There wasn't an easy route around his question. "No...I don't have any employment plans as of yet."

"A person who fails to plan, plans to fail. Since you haven't designed an objective for yourself, let me educate you on what the law expects of you while on parole. As a convicted drug offender, you must submit a weekly urine sample."

"Cool...I don't get high."

"And you also have to find a job or a toothbrush and pillow within thirty days."

The last two items multiplied confusion. "...A toothbrush... pillow?"

Mr. Bart gave a harsh look. "That means you'll be going back to prison if you remain unemployed."

Bradshaw finally lined his thoughts in a single file, grumbling, "With me having a felony, it'll probably take a little more time to find steady work. Employers don't be tryna hire dudes with criminal records. Can't you extend it to at least sixty days?"

"No!" The parole officer proudly shouted, closed the folder, and slipped into silence.

Bradshaw assumed the white guy felt niggers were born to be prisoners. "This shit is crazy."

Though anger had no place in professionalism, Mr. Bart responded with attitude. "What's crazy is guys like you come home and think the system owes them something. In jail, you didn't have to pay for food, electricity, or room and board; us hard-working tax payers foot the bill. Now you expect us to continue to hold your hand. You're just a bunch of talk, no action, one step from getting your brains blown out on a drug corner."

Bradshaw objected, "You got me wrong."

A wry smile almost appeared. "I know your type by the eyes, and it's just a matter of time before you're violated. You won't last. Bet'cha."

Bradshaw heard enough. "Can I go?"

Mr. Bart snapped out of his zone, scrubbed his long hair back with three fingers, then stood. Their initial visit was concluded with

19

his traditional closing remarks, "Ill see you next week on Monday. Good luck. Don't hesitate to contact me if you get shot or arrested."

Thoroughly pissed off, Bradshaw approved by looking towards the direction of the door.

$ $ $ $

Fatigued after such a lengthy wait in the car, Irvin anxiously whipped in the opposite direction from the parole building. "What them coons say?"

Preferring not to relive all the negativity he just endured, Bradshaw kept it simple, "They want me to put my dick in a cup once a week."

"Damn," Irvin looked displeased, "that sucks. Welcome to the sober life."

He shrugged, leaning back in the passenger seat. "And I got to immediately find a job; they stressing that the most."

"If you don't mind gettin' your hands dirty, I know a gig—"

Bradshaw based on Irvin, "Yo, I told you I ain't fucking around!"

The boy kept his cool. "Chill...this some legit shit."

He had Bradshaw's attention.

"Manney-El owe me. I'm one hundred percent sure I could get chu in."

"You talking about that garbage truck joint?"

Irvin grinned. "Yup."

A sigh of relief was expelled. "Hook it up. I can do that until something better comes through."

The boy got on the phone and worked his magic.

With Bradshaw's job situation now secure, his next step was finding a stable place to rest his head. His mother's apartment was fine as an address to put on file, but, by any opinion, the environment meant stagnation. Bradshaw was the only son out of four kids. Since his mother and father were bona fide dope addicts, he was forced to provide for his little sisters.

Kenya and Keema were twins, only thirteen when he got busted.

Trifling rumors spreaded around the hood about the two; therefore, they were now on the wild side. Kia was only one year younger than him, yet very ambitious. At twenty-nine years of age, with hard work and dedication, she was set to graduate from Georgetown's Law School in just a couple of weeks.

If she swam through the blood of the ghetto and made it to dry land, so could he. It wasn't as impossible as trended to believe.

When Bradshaw was dropped off in front of the 107 Building, Irvin said, "I'll be back after I make ah run. Give me two hours, tops."

Bradshaw retrieved his clothes from the trunk and responded with a head nod as the Lexus vanished. One glance at his mother's high-rised building brought back countless memories, good and bad. The front fence that ran from the third to the twelfth floor made the high-rised building take on the likeness of a penitentiary housing unit. It never looked that way to him during childhood, or maybe this was just his first time actually analyzing it. By the harsh smell and heavy foot traffic, he knew nothing changed.

Lugging three large bags inside the building, Bradshaw interrupted a dice game. Shocked to see the face of a ghetto legend, the gamblers greeted him with respect. Bradshaw slid into the fish-canned elevator and got off on the seventh floor. His mother's middle apartment was right next to the play area and elevator lobby. Not much to his surprise, the door was wide open. He walked straight inside to Keema sitting on the couch, playing with the house phone.

"You still funny looking," Bradshaw teased.

Keema turned to the sound of his voice. "Brad!" she squeeled, jaw dropping, racing for a hug.

He held Keema tight, taking in her new look. Her hair and nails were well kept. This wasn't the thirteen-year-old he remembered. His baby sister had matured into womanhood. "Haven't had one of these hugs from you ina long time."

"I'm so happy you home. These fake ass niggas in trouble now."

He ignored her last statement, only responding to the first, "Yeah, I'm happy to be home, too."

Noticing the bags, their warm hug ended. She almost yanked the bags from his grip. "What chu got?"

"Irv hooked me up," Bradshaw answered, eyes shooting around the apartment. He was disheartened by the poor condition. The only furniture in the living room was a couch and one lawn chair where the television used to be. The kitchen had dirty dishes stacked up to the shoulders, roaches crawling up and down the walls.

"Where's Kenya?"

Still inspecting the content within the bags, Keema replied without concern, "Doing her."

"Ma here?"

"She in her room."

Bradshaw headed down the short hall leading to his mother's domain.

He tapped on the closed door not knowing what to expect.

"Keema," Cathy shouted out in a weak tone, "if you ain't got no coins to get me well, get the hell away."

"Ma...it's me, Bradshaw," he whispered, ear almost to the door.

Joy rose her voice, "Boy, you better bring your ass in here!"

He entered the room, totally let down by what he saw. His mother used to be a dime, one of the baddest women in the projects, but years of heroin abuse finally took its toll. Now Cathy was confined to a tattered bed, looking like a bag of bones. She was visually ill. "Hello Ma."

Reaching her arms out, she said, "Come give me some sugar."

Bradshaw fell into his mother's soft touch, giving her a kiss on the cheek. He blamed one man for her downfall. ""Where's Earl?"

"You know your father likes to lie, cheat and con. That dirt-bag-motherfucker is probably out hitting somebody's stash."

The mere thought of his poor-excuse-for-a-father brought on frustration, but he bit the bullet. "Ma, I need to stay here for awhile, until I get my own spot. The parole people need me to keep a steady address."

"What's going on with Peaches?"

"Fuck that bitch."

Cathy let that derogatory statement fly by her head. Pleased to assist her son, she smiled without objection. "You can stay here as long as you need.

The twins share the other bedroom, but the living room can be yours. Wish I had more to offer you."

Bradshaw was grateful. "You're good. Something is better than nothing."

This time his dope-sick mother was the one doing the kissing. "I'm glad you home."

$ $ $ $

Complacency begun to set in after his first shit, shower and shave. Bradshaw attempted to hit his hair with the razor and comb, but, instead of furring his own rug, he decided to spend the last ten dollars on a fresh cut. Even though he was broke, no need to look like it. Against his better judgment, shinning from head to toe, Bradshaw headed to the neighborhood barbershop. On the way he noticed how the corners weren't congested with hustlers pumping product; however, there were numerous junkies dashing in and out of all three high-rise buildings. Whatever illegal activity was going on, the setup was discrete.

On a quick glimpse, Bradshaw saw a dozen of unfamiliar faces when he entered the shop, but the barber at the first chair recognized him immediately.

"Yeah-it-be-dat Bradshaw." howled Jake.

"What's up my dude?" he spat back. As they dapped, Bradshaw briefly reminisced on how Jake and him used to book females downtown. In this ardent contest to see who could get the most phone numbers as kids, Jake's pretty-boy ass was always the victor.

The two were childhood friends who grew away from each other; nevertheless, the love was subtle, yet still there.

Jake instructed, "Have a seat. I got chu on'na house."

Bradshaw obliged, "Good looking."

While being prepped for the free cut, he took a more thorough look around the shop, spotting Tim-Tim. This guy used to sell coke for him and Grub back in the day. Tim-Tim's partner in crime, Willie D, was also posted up. Bradshaw figured the pair were still getting to the papers together. They acknowledged him by throwing up a fist as a symbol of respect.

As the barber got to work on his head, the clippers weren't the only thing buzzing in Bradshaw's ear. Jake schooled him on all he missed while pinched. Almost at the end of the cut, Grub bopped through the door. At six foot and black as tar, the obese man could have been a body-double for Biggie Smalls. Bradshaw and Grub was once thick as thieves, but now Bradshaw had to bite his own fist to resist knocking the fat man's dick-string loose. He sized Grub up, digging the Versace apparel and diamond flooded Rolex. His majestic aura was that of a millionaire.

Grub was stunned seeing Bradshaw. "My nigga, homeboy till the end. You should'a let me know you was out. I would'a painted the town for you."

Bradshaw masked his anger with a chuckle. "I ain't want nobody making a big deal over me coming home."

Grub seemed antsy. "We got to rap when you get finished."

"That we do," Bradshaw agreed.

$ $ $ $

Around twenty minutes later...

Grub was stuffed behind the wheel of a convertible Bentley as the sun brilliantly reflected off of its platinum paint job. Bradshaw realized Grub was on a whole different level game wise, counting it as a rookie mistake to make the kingpin nervous; however, he still brandished a poker face, slipping into the car. "What it is?"

Grub dapped Bradshaw as if he'd just rubbed shoulders with him yesterday. "Ain't no real words to my song, just riddin' to the beat."

As much as Bradshaw didn't want to bring up the past, he straight up asked, "Yo, before we go any further, why you left me hangin' in the joint? That was some buster shit. You was suppose to hold me down."

Grub looked away. "I ain't really got no excuse. Out of sight, out of mind. As you can see, I got caught up out here."

"What part of the game is dat?"

"The part where I got selfish, but I want to clean the slate between us."

Bradshaw didn't go for it. "If a snake bites you once, he'll do it again because it's in his nature."

Grub quickly pitched back, "I know I didn't get at you like I should have, but, Brad, look around. I built an empire for you and I. Couldn't have done it without your ground work. You my ace-boon-coon, and I need your muscle back out here with me."

Bradshaw blurted with absolute certainty, "I'm done. The game ain't for me...too much crutty shit and fake people."

Grub could sense the animosity and didn't want any future problems.

"We better than this."

"Save your breath. The hatchet is buried, past is what it is. To you be your way, to me be mine."

"Respect," said the Biggie look-a-like. "But for the record, you'll always have a spot in my organization. If you ever need a favor, I got chu. That's the least I can do."

Through with the conversation, Bradshaw concluded as he hit the eject button, "I'll keep that in mind."

CHAPTER 2

Peaches and Doobie were standing in front of the 107 building when Bradshaw cut the corner. The paternal bond between father and son immediately overrode everything else, at least for the moment. "Come here, boy!"

"Daddy!" shouted Doobie from a short distance.

Both raced toward each other until their bodies collided. Doobie was lifted off his feet and spun in a circle like a heartfelt scene from a movie with a happy ending. Bradshaw couldn't believe how lanky and tall his son was.

"You got so damn big."

Doobie spoke in a coy manner, "I'm the littlest kid in my class."

Bradshaw pecked him on the forehead. "But I bet you are the smartest, too."

The boy cut to the chase, "Are you coming to live with us?"

Right then he felt terrible his baby's mother ruined their happy home. "I can't, son."

Doobie looked completely disappointed. "Why?"

"That's between me and your mother. But if it makes you feel better, you can come stay with me when I get my own spot."

Sadness conquered Doobie's face.

Witnessing the pain she caused, Peaches couldn't stand herself for being so weak; however, holding a man down for six long years, falling short on the last twelve months, she figured, was worthy of acknowledging her good intentions. Deep inside she understood the victory is never given to the swift, but to the contestant who endured to the finish line. Peaches drew close to him in a desperate way. "Can we talk?"

He disgruntly asked, "About what?"

She sighed and pouted, "Us."

Bradshaw loaned her the cold shoulder. "We already had _ that discussion yesterday."

Doobie's eyes bounced from Daddy to Mommy.

She tried not to cry in front of their child. "We're both adults; can't we work this out?"

Right in the middle of her plea, pointing his fingers like a gun, Irvin eased up from the side. If he was a real shooter, the family of three would have been splattered. Irvin gave a sinister smirk. "Caught ya'll sleepin'."

Startled just a pinch, Bradshaw stepped forward. "You could give a nigga bad nerves creepin' like that."

Still in the thicket of her emotions, Peaches forced herself into a swift greeting, "Hello."

On the strength of what Bradshaw said about how she crossed him, Irvin ignored her dry salutation, giving Doobie a high-five. He turned to his big homie. "Brad, we gotta dip. I need your assistance."

Without so much as a mustard seed of resistance, wanting to get away from his baby's mother, Bradshaw blessed Doobie with a goodbye hug and whispered something in his ear.

Peaches caught the drift. "Oh, you just gone leave? We were holding an important conversation."

Bradshaw took pride in straightening her out. "You do the talking; I'll do the walking. You left me when I was in the can. This is how I felt."

She yanked his sleeve. "Don't play me like this."

"You played yourself." He freed himself. "Now pardon my back."

"Fine." Peaches angrily pulled Doobie away and pranced down the street.

Bradshaw was amused at watching her speed off towards the direction of the bus stop. He actually stood there until the two were no longer in sight. That was his own way of making sure they safely made it out the projects.

Irvin tapped him on the shoulder to break the trance. "Aly, I was gonna drive, but I figured we bop up to the school. It's only four blocks."

Bradshaw didn't like how Irvin's voice sounded. "What school?"

"City Springs."

"For what? School over for the day."

Irvin explained, "I got to make a quick move with a little dude up

Perkins. He's gonna meet me there. I've been helping shorty out."

While Lafayette was to the north of Flag, Perkins was to the east. The difference between Lafayette having six high-rised buildings and Flag having three, Perkins were all low-rises, and that small project alone was just as dangerous as Lafayette Projects and Flag Projects combined. "You know I ain't trying to be around that shit. I'm staying legit."

Irvin retorted, "Them dudes up there shady. I can use an extra pair of eyes. I wouldn't put you in harms way. It'll be quick, please, Bro."

Recounting all the times Irvin never let him down, he was the one person Bradshaw couldn't deny. The man relented with a grind of the teeth.

"Okay. I'll roll with you this time, but don't make it a habit."

"I won't." Irvin was relieved to have his big dawg come along.

Flag House Projects was like a small town always in need of a sheriff to maintain order. In a concrete jungle where only the strong survived, most of the hood stuck together, unless two parties were beefing over drug turf. In those instances, prison or death were mediators. All three buildings were puttied with hundreds of knicked bricks from stray bullet holes and gun fights.

Once the bloody crime scenes cleared, bare-footed children resumed recreational activities. Murder became the norm; drugs was the fuel that kept the spirit of the slums ablazed, and constant drama was a never ending saga.

At one point the playground represented a hangout spot for pushers and fiends, but that evening the basketball courts were empty as Bradshaw and Irvin cut through. They hit a split behind the low-rises that led straight to Pratt Street. Their few minute walk to the school was too short to even be considered an exercise. Bradshaw couldn't believe he was en route to participate in a drug deal. His only concern was not getting knocked off. The thought made him edgy.

When they entered the school grounds, an albino teen, wearing a patch over his right eye, stood alone near a bench. The squalid outfit chosen for the occasion was tailored for a fellow twice his size. He had a flat face, hooked nose. A primary feature that stood out was his big lips. Overlooking Bradshaw, he gave Irvin a pound and said, "Yo, dat coke some straight drop. Dim junkies lovin' it. I need you to throw me in ah extra ounce."

"Lunchbox," Irvin cooled the hyper kid down, "you know Sparky don't want you hustling. I told you from the beginning dat we gonna start off small and stay dat way. You're still learning the basics of this game. Making smart coins and laying back...that's the only way I'll keep fronting you work."

Lunchbox rolled his eyes and sucked his teeth, mugging Bradshaw for no apparent reason. His focus then snapped back to Irvin. "I'm not worried about what my cousin think or say; I wanna be a big-time drug dealer. You can't be bluffin' out here 'cause the judge gonna still give you the whole time when they catch your ass. So why not go hard!"

Disregarding Lunchbox's view, Irvin declined his head, scratching a brow. "You got the money?"

Bradshaw stayed quiet, reading the frustration on the teen's face.

Lunchbox smacked the bread in Irvin's palm. "You ack like you got a roach in your ear while I'm talkin'. But that's okay. Soon as I

34

get my lead check and blow up, I might be the nigga frontin' you. Watch."

Irvin counted the money and handed him the tiny package. "You say the same shit every time we do business. I'll believe it when I see it. You need to work on not spending up all your profit on weed. Treat yourself to a shower and some new gear."

Lunchbox dismissed him by walking off. He shouted without looking back, "Hit chu when I'm finished."

Irvin found him funny. "Remember what I said!"

Bradshaw studied the fast transaction and found several major violations, but he stayed in his own lane and kept it to himself. He was just glad the deal was over.

$ $ $ $

In the 126 building, across from the elevator lobby, was a brick cubicle known as the play area. With a stairway on each end of the hallway, the play area divided the long corridor into two short ramps. In that play area Grub, Tim-Tim, Willie D, Yancy and Kavy held a secret powwow concerning Bradshaw. Even though he was now out of jail and the drug game, it was still something about Bradshaw's demeanor that troubled the fat man.

Labeling Tim-Tim and Willie D as straight suckers, Grub turned to his two prized shooters, handing Yancy a rusty burner. "That's a throw-away joint."

Yancy was a puny dude with a sharp jaw line, trigger finger being the strongest muscle in his body. "Consider it done. Want for something else."

Grub looked at Kavy. "You get rid of the biscuit when it's over. Toss it in the Harbor."

Kavy's tight jeans and ugly face wasn't as unattractive as his attitude. A natural sly disposition would have made him a master of deception had he been born an insect. "Say less, no one will ever find the gun."

Grub rubbed his palms together like a fat kid plotting on a plate of pastries. "Sounds like a plan."

Tim-Tim stood stiff, appalled over Grub jumping to conclusions. Tall and smooth, hair in short corn-rolls, he kept it funky, "Bradshaw ain't no threat. The street knows him from being a man of his word. If Yo say he out the game, I believe it. 1 don't think this the right move."

"I don't pay you to think," replied Grub.

Willie D donned a pair of designer shades for so long that even he forgot they weren't medicated. For a chubby guy with a pot-belly and small bottom, he wore that wear. Backing his crutty buddy,

Willie D uttered, "Boss, Tim-Tim is on point. Maybe we're moving too fast. First give it a few weeks to see what's on his mind. It could be nothing. If you'd get rid of him in a breeze, really for no reason, how do we know you won't snap one day and do the same to us? Besides, you and him like family being that you fuck wit' cho peoples. On the strength of that alone, you should postpone the hit."

Grub paused, weighing the whole matter. Perhaps he was wrong on his end, revealing an inner-weakness better shielded. Since the most important quality of a boss was to reward loyalty with loyalty, it would be detrimental to expose cross in his blood. A fair and balanced leadership was indispensable to the further success of his underworld enterprise. With Yancy and Kavy still in go-mode, Grub cooled down, reconsidering the previous order given. "We don't have to smoke him yet, but I want ya'll to keep ears to the street. Irvin's his little man, and we already know what shorty into. Any word of Bradshaw bumpin' with him on the money tip, especially after he turned my offer down, it's back on like popcorn."

The shooters weren't in agreement, but they did what they were told. Since Tim-Tim and Willie D were plugged into Grub long before them, Yancy and Kavy had no choice but to respect their seniority by exercising silence.

Tim-Tim was the last to utter, "If I'm wrong, [Il kill him myself."

Pleased to have the situation stamped, Grub doled his approval with a slow nod.

$ $ $ $

"You sure this what chu wanna do?" Irvin asked, double-parked in front of Peaches' house.

Bradshaw looked on in concentrated thought. As his mind toured through the memories of the past, Peaches' smile was the guide. She did big right for him until falling to the wayside. Some females would have dipped from the beginning; at least she hung tough through some of his hardest years. No matter who Peaches fucked behind his back, she not once neglected Doobie. Bradshaw had to give her credit for being a wonderful mom if nothing else. Though feeling betrayed, he still loved Peaches. "I won't get nowhere draggin' on her. She might take it out on my son. To listen to her side...] owe her that much. Plus I whispered to Doobie I'd swing by tonight."

Irvin understood where he was coming from. "You chillin' over here?"

Bradshaw answered, "I'm unsure. Either way, I'll make it to my mom's house if Peaches starts trippin'. I don't want you outside waiting on me while you on the grind. Time is money."

"I can dig it. Here..." Irvin broke off a couple hundred out of the paper he got from Lunchbox. He slid it to his big homie. "That's a little something for you to catch a cab or whatever."

"I'm good." Bradshaw attempted to hand back the drug money.

Irvin insisted, "Nah, that's also your cut for going with me to the school. Like you said, time is money."

Bradshaw humbled himself, taking the situation for what it was.

"I'll scoop you from work tomorrow so we can celebrate your first day.

"Good looking."

"You Already."

Bradshaw got out of the car and settled himself for the mission at hand. His watch stood still as he knocked. Peaches disrupted a second set of knocks by easing the door ajar. She was in a bathrobe, eyes puffy as if they'd been marinating in tears. Staring at her in a mindless silence, he couldn't ignore her enchantment, how a long, rich grain of natural hair cascaded down her shoulders. Every delightful curve was visible. Peaches broke the silence.

"What do you want?"

Bradshaw kept his heart. "Where's Doobie?"

"Sleep."

She tried to shut the door, but he stopped it with a foot. "Doobie's isn't the only reason I'm here. Can I come in?"

Peaches answered by stepping aside. "I guess you came to watch me cry."

"No. actually brought my ears with me."

His response was one she didn't expect. Assuming she now had his attention, Peaches made her case. "I know I'm in the wrong, but I was also faithful to you for six whole years. I just got caught up in a moment of weakness. That don't mean I stopped loving you."

"Why didn't you tell me? I would've understood. We're friends before anything. Love don't lie. You built yourself into a superwoman, had me hootin' and hollerin' about how faithful you were. You made a nigga think you was on a certain level, so I held you to that standard."

Peaches called his past faults into account. "You cheated on me with that bitch, Shavon, when I was pregnant, but I forgave you."

Bradshaw justified his actions. "That was so long ago I don't even remember. You're being petty."

She flipped out. "Yeah the fuck right. I don't know what you want from me, but I'm not kissing your ass."

His ego got involved. 'Forget it. I came to rap, but you wanna fight."

As he went for the door, Peaches realized she played her hand wrong. The woman rushed her baby's father with a hug from behind. "I was just talking out of my head. Please, baby, don't go. I'm lost without you."

It was in that second he desired to stay the night. "You got one more time to act like I'm the villain, and I'm out."

Since she felt any verbal outburst would cause him to leave, body language was chosen as the proper communicative tool to get her point across. Peaches quickly spun him around, laboring to find his lips. Through Bradshaw's clenched teeth, she gave aggressive tongue action until his jaw loosened up. It was then she dragged her baby's father into the bedroom.

"What are you doing?" he asked, dick growing rapidly.

Passion filled her vocal cords. "I want you to beat it up. I been a bad girl."

Just when his mouth was about to refuse, the thought came he should fuck the woman for payback to show her what she was missing. That would be soothing, even refreshing to his spirit. He pushed her onto the bed.

Peaches yanked him on top of her, and that's when the fireworks went off. They made love like two animals in the wild. Bradshaw couldn't deny the intensity.

After their steamy session, Peaches asked as her head rested on his chest, "So what's your plans? These streets ain't right."

He freely expounded, "I already got a job with Manny-El."

That revelation amused her. She proceeded in folly, hoping to gain a smile, "Your gonna beee a dirty traaashman."

Bradshaw immediately became annoyed by her reaction, "What's all that for?"

Struggling not to laugh, she answered, "That's so unlike you. Manny- El and them are fiends, sales. Everyone knows that. You're a boss. I can see you owning a dump like that, not working for one."

Bradshaw thought the idea over for a second. "Got to crawl before you walk."

Sensing he was self-conscious about the issue, she added, "But I'm proud of you, though. Doing it the right way...I see it as a great example for Doobie."

The two closed a few open wounds by talking matters out. Neither could remember exactly when sleep overcame them.

$ $ $ $

That morning Bradshaw awoke to his son's smile. "Hey, tiger," he said, adjusting his eyes to the sun beaming through the window.

Doobie still had on his pajamas. "You live with us again?"

Bradshaw didn't want to get Doobie's hopes up. "I just kept my word and dropped in last night. You ain't think I was gonna lie to you...did you?"

The boy giggled. "You never lie."

Bradshaw looked at the clock. "Go get ready for school."

Doobie complied.

A kiss and a smack on the ass snatched Peaches out of her coma.

Thirty minutes after a quick shower, Doobie was dropped off early enough to catch the school's breakfast. Bradshaw made it to the garbage lot on time. Peaches inquired as the man exited the cab, "Are you coming home tonight?"

He responded in an evasive manner, "Haven't thought that far, but the only home I know is my mother's house for now."

Peaches was speechless, signaling for the cab driver to pull off.

Bradshaw was feeling himself. Wearing the pussy out gave him the advantage, and he planned to make her yearn for him until she went crazy. *That was exactly how he felt when the shoes were on the other foot.* Once the cab shot left, Bradshaw walked into the job prepared for whatever in store. The oppressive smell hit him, but he fought through the stench. With this being his first real job, he wanted to make a good impression.

Manny-El was the supervisor. This fifty-year-old man always reminded him of Grady off Fred Sanford. The only thing Manny-El looked more tougher. Following a phony ass orientation, Bradshaw was assigned to a four-man team. This crew was responsible for the whole York Road area. On the road at 8:00 sharp, Manny-El drove the truck while the others collected trash. Bradshaw recognized

43

each one of the dudes on his detail. Just as Peaches mentioned, the three were crack heads he used to serve. They kept eyes on Bradshaw the entire day until he cleared the air by telling them he had no drugs. Needless to say, they were thoroughly disappointed.

By 2:00 p.m., their route was done. The crew described the work load as light. Bradshaw hated to think what a heavy day consisted of. At quitting time, enjoying the positive feeling that came after an honest days work, Irvin was out front in the Lexus.

Bradshaw hopped in the car exhausted. "I'm tired as shit."

Irvin sighed, "You stink."

"I know. I'm overdue for a hot shower."

"How was it?"

"Not all that bad, nasty," explained Bradshaw. "I guess it's just another form of dirty money."

The young man chuckled. "You met Isaiah yet?"

"Who?" It was his first time hearing the name.

"The boss. He the old head who run all that shit."

"Nah. Should I be pressed to meet him?"

"Not really. Yo just cool peoples. He like to promote niggas who bust their ass on the job."

Bradshaw was so beat at that moment he cared less about a raise. "I'll cross that bridge when it comes."

The ride to the projects was short. The hood was alive when the Lexus stopped in front of the 107 building. Irvin said, "I'll grab you later. Tina tryna see you."

Bradshaw nodded. "Bet."

The pair parted.

As he wearily trudged into the building, the young dealers acknowledged his presence. Ever since moving with his mother, Bradshaw noticed the drug trade in Flag House had boomed. Old habits died hard, but he was striving to maintain his new walk. He just didn't anticipate the temptation would be this great. Theorizing a positive stride sounded good when putting his blueprint together in a cell, but to execute that plan took more than words or a few cognitive certificates. This was where theory met practice.

Both twins were on the couch when he entered the apartment. Kenya inspected her brother with a curled upper lip. He mugged back, forcing the girl into a hug. "What's up, Ken. You ain't gonna show your brother love?"

"Yuk, you smell like rotten eggs." She pushed him away with disgust.

"So do that perm ya'll females use."

Keema playfully prompted, "No perm we ever used reeked like you do now. Bro, you need to handle that."

Bradshaw couldn't refute the girls were absolutely correct. On his way to hop into the water, he tripped off of how mature his sisters got.

A hot shower later, shadowed by five extra minutes used to groom his waves in the bathroom mirror, Keema was now on the couch alone. Bradshaw asked, "Damn, where Kenya go so fast?"

Keema dispassionately answered, "She in the room. Some company came over while you were getting your hygiene straight."

It took Bradshaw a second to grasp the idea. Every dude in the projects knew better to be sweet on any of his sisters before he caught time. He personally felt disrespected. "What...you mean she got a nigga back there?"

Keema scowled, not really computing the reason why he was exerting so much energy.

By her offhanded reaction, he knew the answer to his question was yes. Still viewing the twins as little girls, not the adult women they'd become,

Bradshaw stalked to the bedroom and banged on the door. "Open this door up before I knock it down!"

Clearly embarrassed by her brother's moronic command, Kenya stormed out the room. "What the fuck is your problem?"

Bradshaw tried to look into the room, but she closed the door. "Do Ma know you got male company?" he roared.

Kenya laughed in his face. "What do you think I am...ah child? You geekin'. I'm grown. I do what I want, when I want to do it. If you got a problem, tough shit!" Leaving her brother on stupid, the girl returned back to her company.

Bradshaw stomped back into the living room, pacing the floor like a hungry lion in a cage. The situation made his head hurt. He looked at Keema, wordless.

She shrugged and turned on a CD player.

$ $ $ $

Bradshaw napped until relieving himself of the headache caused by Kenya. He got up and phoned Irvin to snatch him as soon as possible. Dressed in Gucci gear, by 9:00 p.m. he was dipped in the passenger seat of the Lexus.

During the ride to Cherry Hill, Bradshaw griped, "I don't know what's up with the twins. I got home from work and Kenya had some coon all up in her room. When I tried to check her, she straight clowned me."

Irvin understood his big homie's dilemma. "I know you wasn't expecting the twins to be doing them, but shit changed. You can't focus on how it was; recognize how it is. Only then can you change the situation."

Out of the many years he schooled his little buddy, now his little buddy was spitting him the game. Apart of him couldn't embrace the truth, but he bit his tongue and allowed Irvin's wise words to resonate. Bradshaw tried to sooth the turbulent thoughts by putting his mind on Tina. *Tonight he would make her vagina feel his pain.* And sure enough at 10:30 pronto, the two were enthralled in *some rigorous sex.* All the work Bradshaw put in to get his nut, slumped him.

Tina never reached her climax, but no man ever fucked her like Slick. She grew to accept that reality for what it was. Banking on using Bradshaw as a substitute until her own man came home from his extortion charge, drenched in sweat, she relaxed in his arms as the two stared at the ceiling. Tina asked, "Boo, what chu doing wit cha time? I know you probably got one of them dope blocks locked down."

"Nah, I work."

She was disappointed, yet intrigued. "What kind of work you do?"

Bradshaw almost gagged getting the words out. "I'm a garbage man."

Tina put him under the spotlight. "You mean to tell me you pick up trash like them thirsty prisoners that be on road crew?"

His question was more like a statement. "Ain't that what trash men do."

She obnoxiously scoffed, "Tell me that you hustle on the side or something. That little bit of money can't be your only income, right?"

He gave her a shitty look.

She sighed. "I always get stuck with a broke ass loser."

Bradshaw's anger took control. "All you hood bitches want a nigga to do is risk his freedom while ya'll benefit. Soon as a nigga go to jail, ya'll split. Then it's off to your next meal ticket. I played that game before. Nice try. If you can't get with me making an honest living, you can keep it moving."

She rolled her eyes. "Oh, don't worry...I am, da fuck."

He shoved her off the bed. "Your gold-digging ass can sleep on the floor."

Without any hesitation, Tina gathered her clothes and left the room.

$ $ $ $

The entire night was ruined over Bradshaw and Tina's spat. Irvin figured it best to take the girls home. Reading Bradshaw's face, the boy knew his friend wanted to smack the shit out of Tina.

Whispering to each other, the two girls giggled in the back seat as Irvin asked, "What the fuck is so funny?"

Forcing a straight face, Candice responded, "Nothing..."

Not satisfied, Irvin warned, using an icy tone, "It better not be nothing because I'll kick both you bitches out my shit!"

In a childish rant, Tina spoke out of turn, "Whattteverrr. We been kicked out of better shit, da fuck."

Irvin slammed on the brakes on the middle of the Handover Bridge.

Pinching her homegirl's arm, Candice petitioned to Irvin, "Why you acting like that?"

Irvin retrieved a pistol from his waist and pointed toward the back seat. "Get out!"

Upon seeing the gun, the girls complied quickly.

Bradshaw was amused.

The Lexus sped off. "I ain't gonna let nobody get out on you. Not no nigga, not no bitch. Fuck that shit. Them ho's got my nigga twisted."

The shocked look on their faces was a portrait to remember. "Them slut's eyes got big as shit when they seen the hammer."

Reliving the moment, both men laughed their asses off.

CHAPTER 3

The next day Bradshaw experienced what coworkers called a heavy load. His crew hauled so much trash he almost quit. He was thoroughly beat once the shift ended. While waiting out front for Irvin to pick him up, Bradshaw ran into the head boss at the gate.

"You must be my new worker," asked Isaiah. He was a scraggly black man in a baseball cap, wearing a crisp blazer and slacks, appearing to be the cleanest thing at the joint.

"Yeah, I'm Bradshaw."

They pressed palms.

"'Manny-El informed me you were on the verge of giving up today."

Amazed how fast word spread at the job, Bradshaw answered honestly, "I thought about it."

Isaiah continued, "Well...don't. This might be a dirty job, but it's a clean living."

With all the negativity that came whenever his new job title was mentioned, Bradshaw responded with a question, "What exactly is a clean living these days?"

He firmly replied, "It's a living that will keep your black ass out of prison. I heard about you, your past, and I think things will pay off so long as you stay focused. This job isn't a glamorous profession fit for everyone. But one man's trash is another man's treasure. Hang in there."

Bradshaw gave the same eye contact he used at the parole hearing. "I feel that, appreciate the motivation."

In the middle of them touching bases, a cab pulled up and out came Peaches.

"Why the fuck you ain't come home last night!" shouted Peaches, walking towards him.

Isaiah could break down the keys to success but not the wrath of a mad black woman. Seeing the rage in her face, he stepped off with the quickness.

Bradshaw took offense to her bringing their personal matters to his job. "Don't approach me like that."

She got louder, "Where was you at last night, huh?"

"My mother's house."

Peaches swung at him, almost connecting before being grabbed. "Liar!"

"You trippin'! He held her hands down. "Swing again, and this conversation is over."

She blocked his path. "I want proof you was there."

He got frustrated. "I don't have a reason to lie, just as much as I don't owe you an explanation. You're not my wife. You ain't give me all this energy when I was locked down 'cause you knew where I was. Don't switch up now. I already got one dick-head parole officer in my ass, surely don't need a second one."

Peaches fell into pieces. "Why are you doing this to me? We already made up."

He checked her, "You ain't the one who got hurt, so it's easy for you to forgive and forget —"

"You fucked Shavon."

"But I was still there for you. I didn't disappear."

"Be there for me now, and don't disappear."

Bradshaw stuck his heart in his back pocket. "I just need some time and space to build the trust back up. That won't happen over night."

Peaches embraced the love of her life. "You can trust me, bae."

"That's what your mouth say."

She tried to pull him to the cab. "Can you come home with me tonight? I just want to be held."

He broke away. "I can't. Me and Irvin got something important lined up, and he on his way to grab me."

Sick of going back and forth, Peaches gave up. "You do what you do, but I won't always be your doormat." With that expressed, she found her way back to the cab and shook ass.

Bradshaw stayed at the job for an extra hour after Peaches left.

Irvin was a no-show, leaving him to ponder his baby mother's words the whole walk home.

$ $ $ $

Earl was at the kitchen fiddling with a needle when his son breezed past him without speaking. As a routine, Bradshaw prepared for a shower by first organizing his clothes. But when he examined his expensive collection, a few bags were missing. Trying not to point fingers, Bradshaw confronted his mother before raising hell. Cathy was inside her room in bra and panties, staring out the window as if searching the sky for a lost dream. Just observing her frailness made Bradshaw despise Earl with all his heart.

"Ma, we need to chat."

Cathy could tell something was on his mind. "What's wrong, son?"

The more he thought about it, the more upset he got. "My little homie took me shopping when I came home, spent a few large bills on my gear. I looked through my stuff, half is gone... shit I didn't even get a chance to sport."

Cathy immediately pardoned herself. "I didn't take it; in fact, I haven't been out of this room since you been back home."

"I'm not accusing you," he compassionately touched her hand, "I'm just suggesting we call a family meeting."

Eavesdropping from the other side of the door, Earl blasted into the room without warning. "Nigga, you need to shut the fuck up. Nobody stole nothing. You blowing my high with all this crying bullshit she don't need to hear."

Bradshaw sized up every inch of his father's track-littered frame. His thin-skinned-ninety pounds was tattooed with abscesses and open scabs. "First of all, no one was talking to you, so take your fiend-ass back into the kitchen and mind your business."

"Shut your mouth in my house!"

Cathy corrected Earl, "No, this is my house, and my son can speak."

Earl gave his wife no airtime, keeping his focus on Bradshaw. "Ain't no thieves in this pad. Nobody want your cheap shit. Regular project people don't even know how to pronounce the names on some of that garbage you had."

"To know so much detail," he got in his father's face, "you went through my shit. I bet you stole it."

Earl stood bold. "Yeah, I saw it but ain't take shit."

Bradshaw lost control and grabbed the man by the neck. The commotion brought the twins into the room. Kenya jumped on Bradshaw's back while Keema struggled to peel his fingers from around Earl's throat.

Even Cathy refereed. Once the two were separated, the mother wedged herself between them.

Earl was flustered by his son's disrespect. He said, "I want you out of this house right now. Take the couch with you!"

Cathy went from referee to peacekeeper, "Earl, stop it! Bradshaw has a right to be mad; his clothes missing. It's only five people in this house. The shit didn't grow legs and walk off on its own. Whoever got it, just give it up."

Earl was still angry that Bradshaw challenged him. "Fuck your clothes. you're not staying another night in this house!"

Kenya spoke for she and Keema. "This is too much confusion. If he never came here, we wouldn't be having this family feud. I agree with daddy, you should leave."

Bradshaw was shocked by Kenya's statement. "I take it you still salty about yesterday. So maybe you stole my shit and sold it for get-back."

Kenya was so offended, she pushed him. "You not the same brother I once looked up to. You ah has been, damn loser. All that money you used to have and now you broke. You not doing us no favor by staying here, bringing nothing to the table. Part of manhood is being intelligent enough to know when you not wanted."

Keema supported her sister by giving her brother dismissive eyes.

Kenya's words cut Bradshaw deep. He could no longer see himself staying there. "Y'all got it...keep them clothes. Just because I'm trying to float straight, y'all disrespect me like this. But y'all wish granted...Ain't got to worry about me no more."

While Cathy went against the rest and pled with him to stay, Earl ran and opened the front door just to be smart. Done with all the extra stress and nonsense, Bradshaw packed his remaining clothes and got out of the apartment as quick as he could. He couldn't believe how bad his family deteriorated. Debating over his limited options of either going to Peaches' house or a shelter, he hit Irvin first.

$ $ $ $

An hour or so later...

Despite offering no explanation for not showing up at the job, Irvin welcomed Bradshaw into his crib. "Yo, what's mine is yours. Had you asked me to chill here from day one, you could'a ducked that whole grudge match at your mother's house. But don't sweat it; you and your clothes are safe here."

Bradshaw was impressed by the condo. Not only was it decked out with expensive furniture, it was spacious and spotless. Anyone who entered Irvin's domain would come to the conclusion that he had some loot on tuck. As Bradshaw was escorted to the extra bedroom, he uttered, "I appreciate you opening up your doors to me. I didn't ask before because I knew you were heavy in them streets. With me on this positive tip, I didn't want to burden you—"

Irvin chopped it there. "You my man, the nigga who showed me how to get money. I owe you. However you chose to live, I got your back no matter if you right or wrong. I would rather have you here with me than any place else. Call this condo your home from now on."

Bradshaw coughed up his first smile since the incident with his family, "You can't imagine how much this mean to me."

"Don't mention it." Irvin brushed it off as a small thing. "This ain't shit. If you wouldn't ever got caged, you'd be where Grub at or farther."

Bradshaw considered the truth of his statement, which motivated him to become inquisitive, "You keep bringing up how good that fat fuck doing, but it don't look like you starving. Give me the real deal."

Never thinking his big homie would ask, Irvin was anxious to go into detail. "Depending on how generous the streets are, I cop a bird or two every month from Grub, but it kills me to fuck witcho knowing what he did to you.

Just so happens he give me the best prices. I ain't gonna stunt, making five or six grand every week had me cozy, but my eyes on a bigger prize right now."

While Bradshaw's sight marveled over his new bedroom, as much as he hated to feed into it, he continued to probe, "I wonder what type of prize would that be?"

Irvin kicked back in a recliner by the bed. "A new connect from Miami want to try me out. If they prove to be true bill, I could finally cut Grub off. It would be triple the work for dirt cheap."

Bradshaw instantly picked up on all the shit Irvin wasn't saying, the dilemma that stood between him and success. "Being in the position to make a power play and branch off, you worried about Grub trying to take you to war?"

"Exactly." Irvin lit a smoke. "I can't trust nobody out here, that's why I move solo. You my mentor, always been, and I could use your muscle. If we put our backs to each other and minds together, there's no telling what we could accomplish with this move. And though it's unfair for me to ask your help, I need you."

The pressure combined with Irvin's despair, along with a chance to crush Grub by breaking even, caused Bradshaw's former life to tug at him. Hustling was the greatest thing he ever knew how to do, one of his best talents. So long as he played an instrumental role by staying in the shadows, he figured no foul, no fault. Besides, Irvin had his mind made up regardless, and the boy would be a dead man the moment he slipped from Grub's empire. Not wanting to see the worst happen to his little homie, Bradshaw spoke against himself, "Since you already got it figured out, I'll role with you, but I don't want my name in nothing. I'm on parole, which means I'm keeping my job, and I won't be seen on the forefront. Just tell me what you need me to do."

Completely happy with Bradshaw's choice, Irvin gave him big dap. "I'm supposed to holla at Miami in a couple of days. Until then, we chill and map out a master plan on how to make this power move work."

The game was filthy, and Bradshaw could only picture the type of drama yet to come; however, now standing by Irvin's side, he braced himself for the unknown.

$ $ $ $

While collecting his thoughts over a fresh cup of mud, Mr. Bart got physically aroused when Spring sashayed into the break room.

Staring at the woman, he licked the realm or his cup and said, "I love my coffee like my woman...dark, creamy and sweet."

His derogatory statement would have been paralyzing if she wasn't already immune to Bart's sexual advances. Spring was a very thin female with a plump backside. In terms of beauty, pretty wasn't the word. Her coworkers were thoroughly convinced she could have earned a better living as a model opposed to a parole officer. She was a total lust magnet for the average male who lacked self-control, which was the reason why Mr. Bart couldn't manage himself whenever in her company.

When she didn't respond, he shot another dart, "It's not an easy chore being overwhelmed with such high caseloads. First it was a matter of every parole officer carrying his or her own weight, now it's a matter of getting more work out of less staff. It could wear an individual out. But if you ever need a private massage, I'd like to be the one to make that happen."

Just the thought of his slimy hands on her body done it for Spring. She could take no more. "Don't you ever get sick of being a sleazebag? Do you not know when to fall back?"

As if he hadn't heard a word she said, Mr. Bart continued to feast with his eyes.

Spring slid a dollar bill inside the vending machine. "Men are dogs..."

He focused on her ass cheeks as she bent over to retrieve the candy bar.

"Will you quit it!" she demanded.

The aggressive tone of voice snapped him out of a daze. "I'm sorry."

He eased toward her like a serpent. "I didn't mean to offend you."

"Sure. You never do." She moved in the opposite direction, interfacing the table between them.

"Give me a break." He downed the cup of coffee, holding his arms out like a sincere friend. "You always take me the wrong way. I only wanted to offer a hand. You look tired."

Spring completely circled around the table as he pursued her. "I'm fine."

Mr. Bart stopped short of making a scene. "Very energetic, aren't

"As you can see," she smiled to ward off the beast, "I'm not beat at all. In fact, I could actually handle a few more clients on my caseload. Instead of you lending me a hand, let me help you."

Not having the slightest clue of what she was talking about, a brow rose. "I'm listening."

"Since you mentioned having a heavy caseload, I'd be happy to lift a particular one off of your hands."

Mr. Bart suspiciously asked, "Which one would that be."

"His name is Bradshaw Peatican, a high risk parolee I can really put the clamp on."

Her request stunk. "This sounds more like a favor. Besides having one less jailbird to watch over, how do I benefit?"

She stuck the candy bar halfway down her throat and pulled it out slowly. "You and I can discuss that at a later date."

After over a year working with Spring, he finally was about to slide to first base. Mr. Bart could feel his cock turning rock hard. "I'll have that file on your desk before the day ends."

"Thank you." Spring slowly turned, seductively switching out of the break room.

Mission accomplished.

$ $ $ $

Bradshaw's first paycheck brought in two hundred-fifty dollars before taxes. Though viewing it as just pennies, he appreciated the hard-earned ration and decided to treat his son. Peaches showed no sign of spite when he called, assuring Doobie would be ready by time he got there. Bradshaw borrowed Irvin's extra whip, which was a fly ass Fleetwood, and sped to his baby- mother's house.

The sun was just sinking when he arrived. Doobie dashed to the car and knocked on the door. Soon as the kid strapped himself into the passenger seat, he revisited the same quiz that had him troubled! "Dad, how come you don't come stay with us for good?"

Assuming Peaches put him up to pose that question, Bradshaw chose his words carefully, "Me and your mother decided to be friends. Two parents don't always have to live together to be happy; some people are better, stronger apart."

As the car effortlessly vanished from the house, Doobie spoke his whole opinion in one statement, "You're mad at mommy because she had a man over."

He honored Doobie's bluntness, refusing to counter with a lie. "Yeah, guess I am a little salty about that."

Surprisingly, the kid supported his father's feelings. "I don't blame you. I would be mad too if my girlfriend cheated on me."

Bradshaw cut his eyes at Doobie. "What you know about having a girlfriend?"

He explained, "I got two girlfriends in school who say they love me, so I go with both of them."

"Whoa...slow down, Casanova. You got it like that, huh?"

The eight-year-old looked away in a coy manner. "I sure do."

Bradshaw's mind was blown at how fast children were nowadays, forgetting how quick he himself came up. The man could only shake his head and smile. "I heard that, but I want you to focus on your school work, that way you can make something of yourself. Don't chase girls, chase money, and girls will chase you. Okay?"

"Alright."

With that understood, the father ruffled his son's hair and turned up the music. The two jammed all the way to the mall. After copping Doobie two nice outfits and a pair of sneaks, they went to the movies. When their outing had expired, followed with a promise to repeat the same program every Friday, Doobie was dropped off by 10:00 p.m. For some reason, Peaches didn't nag this time: instead, the woman just waved from the porch and took her son inside the house.

Bradshaw was actually pleased, heading to the condo in a peaceful state of mind.

CHAPTER 4

The weekend wasn't hitting on nothing. Monday rolled around in what seemed like overnight, which meant it was time to see Mr. Bart's miserable ass again; Bradshaw used his break to do so. Armed with a pay- stub, he checked into the parole office. At the snap of a finger, much faster than the initial visit, his name was called by a female this time. Wondering who she was, Bradshaw followed her to the back.

During the short stroll, the woman brought him up to speed. "I'm Ms. Rice, and I'! be handling your case from here out."

Bradshaw gave a skeptical nod, spellbound by her walk. The stranger's complexion could best be described as butterscotch. A lack of makeup exposed her natural beauty. Long dark hair ran down her back like a chocolate waterfall. A sharp nose hid her cheek bones, giving a youthful appeal. Completely smitten by his new parole officer, Bradshaw admired her coke- bottle figure.

Once inside the office, without a moments delay, she flopped behind the desk and got down to business. "Have you found a job yet, Mr. Peatican?"

Bradshaw pulled out the pay stub, making note to himself that she wasn't wearing a ring. He would break an arm to have her.

She returned the pay stub. "You are scheduled to submit a weekly urinalysis. You have not been under the influence of any drugs, I hope?"

"No. I'm clean," Bradshaw assured.

"Are you ready to submit your sample?"

"Sure," he responded.

"Good."

As she prepped for testing, he said, "Can I ask you something?"

She looked up, "Feel free."

Bradshaw took a dry swallow. "Are you single?"

Concealing an oncoming blush, she replied, "What does that have to do with anything?"

"Because I would love to take you out."

Her response was evasive, "You have a piss test to do at the moment, so let's focus on that." She handed him the sample container.

He gave a charming smile. "At least it wasn't a no."

She quickly quipped, "It wasn't a yes either."

Yella was a freckl-faced hustler from Park Heights. Groomed by straight killers, he played no games, This outspoken teenager had enough street credibility, drugs and guns to put the press on any opposition that stood in his way. Not a soul in the Baltimore region was gutsy enough to challenge him; therefore, he did what he want, when and wherever he wanted to do it. Moreover, shorty was the shit out Park Heights, ruling the Westside neighborhood with an iron fist.

In a peach Range on Denmore Avenue, slobbering on Yella's manhood, Kenya bobbed her head with force. Since he claimed to never have a moment to waste, Kenya knew that if she made him cum fast, he'd throw in an extra ten bucks on top the usual fifty for her lip service. Preferring to deal only with big-shot hustlers, making them pay to play was her thing. But out of all the niggas Kenya was fucking, Yella was the one she clung to the most, sometimes even letting him smash for free.

Yella boo loved with his main bitch while catching the head. "You know I love you, right?"

Melissa shouted into the phone, "Why the fuck you sound all sleepy and relaxed? That car is too quiet...like...like you in a bedroom or something."

"You trippin'." Yella motioned for Kenya to eat him up faster.

Melissa remained suspicious. "I don't trust you."

"I don't have a reason to lie." He stuffed his pole down Kenya's throat until she nearly choked. "So, if I opened the windows or turned the music up, would that make you feel better?"

"Nope," she pouted.

Kenya went to work on the dick, preparing herself to catch his babies.

In the mist of his own excitement, Yella put on a sad tone, "It's not healthy takin' an honest man through unnecessary insecurities. Don't no bitty want me but you. The whole world knows I'm yours."

Melissa fed into his false concept. "Tell me you love me."

Kenya felt him about to explode.

"I love you."

If he did have a broad around him, assuming it would make the female uncomfortable, Melissa demanded, "Say it louder!"

Then came the hot cum.

"I loooove you! Shit! I love you so fuckin' much."

Melissa was satisfied. "That's better. And I love you, too."

Yella slowly zipped his jeans and slid Kenya a weak twenty dollar bill, giving a sly wink that ensured he would hit her off with more on a later date.

Merely pleased to be in his pocket and have one up on Melissa, Kenya proudly accepted the cash without a fuss.

$ \qquad $ \qquad $ \qquad $

Using the felonious excuse of having a long wait at the parole office, Bradshaw took the rest of the evening off from work. With nothing else really on his agenda, he headed to the barbershop to get a touch up. When he got there, the spot was packed with a lot of Grub's flunkies. Jake's chair was the only one open, and that's where he plopped himself down. "What's up homeboy?"

Jake gave a snappy response, "Same cat, different mouse."

"An empty chair is a bad sign. Good as you cut, thought you'd have mad clientele."

Jake draped the cape around Bradshaw. "Naw, my clientele off the chain. Grub is on his way to get a trim. He don't like nobody else cutting his wig but me. Whenever he needs a cut, he prefer I keep the chair available until

I'm done with him, which chops my booth rent in half. He is the boss, and I don't want to get on his bad side, so I'll have to make your cut quick."

Bradshaw wanted so bad to say *fuck that Fat-son-of-a-bitch*, but he responded by not responding at all. Nevertheless, the expression on his face said a thousand words.

Not in agreement with how Grub carried Bradshaw greezy when shit went down, he, too, was one who prayed on Grub's downfall. Jake could only feel Bradshaw's pain.

In the middle of the cut, Grub bopped into the shop with Bradshaw's sister, Kia, in tow. The big guy's eyes magnetically locked onto Bradshaw.

Exhibiting a composed demeanor, Grub said, "Even in changed men, some things remain the same. I see you still like to stay groomed. If it was anybody but you occupying my seat, I would have turned this barbershop upside down."

Bradshaw couldn't mask his own befuddlement. He bluntly asked, "What yall doing together?"

Kia pecked her brother on the cheek. "I thought you heard me and Calvin are engaged."

Bradshaw grilled Grub. "Yo, why you ain't tell me you was fuckin' with my sister, about to marry her?"

Grub gave a wry grin. "We been together for five years now. Surprise surprise."

To prevent steam from shooting out of her brother's ears, she calmed him by asking, "Are you okay?"

She had to be aware that Grub left him high and dry. However, at the verge of exploding, he answered in a balanced tone, "I'm cool...okay as long as you happy."

Not taking her eyes off of Bradshaw, Kia hugged Grub lovingly. "I'm perfect; I knew you'd understand."

In fear that something was about to pop off, Jake rushed the rest of Bradshaw's cut.

Outside the shop, Bradshaw spoke with his sister in private. "What the hell do you see in him?"

Her eyes rolled to the side as she said, "Calvin treats me like a queen. He also paid my way through law school. What dude you know does that for a woman he don't love?"

Though she had a point, Bradshaw sighed dejectedly. He saw how his sister doted over Grub inside the barbershop. She was truly in love. He somehow seen the new development as a two-way street, a give and take. Bradshaw realized he could actually use their situation to his advantage. "If that's where your heart is, as your brother, I have no choice but to respect your decision."

Kia was elated and relieved, giving him a tight hug. "Thanks. And welcome home."

Before they went their separate ways, both exchanged numbers, promising to not be strangers.

$ \qquad $ \qquad $ \qquad $

An undisclosed amount of time later...

Bradshaw entered the condo and was surprised to see a scantily-clad young woman lounging on the couch. She was attractive, dark complexioned, voluptuous curves. A silk robe barely concealed her assets.

Sweeping the length of long cornrows over one shoulder, she nonchalantly glanced at him and said, "You must be Bradshaw?"

He became defensive. "Who are you?"

Her tone was that of an old friend. "Vanessa."

"Where's Irvin?"

She opened the robe to expose a set of flawless tits. "Your guess is just as good as mine."

Bradshaw imagined her to be one of Irvin's play toys, but to be left inside the condo alone, her value had to be greater. "If I wasn't sharp, I would swear you're attempting to come onto me."

She spoke seductively, "I thought it would be nice if you joined me on the couch before Irvin gets back in. We can make it quick."

"I'm not interested; put some clothes on." Bradshaw turned away and walked towards the direction of the kitchen. As soon as he stepped into the threshold of the dining room, there Irvin was sitting at the table with a huge quantity of cocaine in front of him.

Irvin laughed. "Peekaboo."

When Vanessa giggled, Bradshaw also smiled. "Jokes on me, huh?"

Irvin responded, "I was only testing your loyalty. If you would creep, you'd steal."

Bradshaw was actually proud of Irvin putting him through the test, which was an old strategy introduced to his student early in the game. He humbled himself and said, "You did right."

As Bradshaw sat at the table, Irvin responded, "You taught me that most dudes are weak for pussy. A bitch could be the death of a real nigga. You never let that come between true friendship, and that's one reason I always looked up to you."

Vanessa closed her robe and continued to lamp on the couch. She flicked through several television channels with the remote, slipping back into her own world as if nothing special was really going on.

Just to think about how Bradshaw's home plan was foundated on the straight and narrow, how he philosophized the many reasons not to get caught up again, now he was in front of a mountain of cocaine without one nervous bone in his body. Bradshaw asked in a hushed tone, "Who is shorty?"

While breaking up large white rocks with a mallet, Irvin answered, "I like to think of her as wifey. She's my new connects niece. Speaking of the plug, he just fronted me these five kilos."

"How much he want back?"

"Fifty grand."

Bradshaw immediately calculated the profit margin. "Ten a bird, not bad."

Irvin explained, "And this is just a test run. Grub was charging me twenty a joint, so this is more like a two-for-one special. Sweet... right?"

"Hell yeah, but how did you meet the plug?"

"Well," Irvin paused for a second, "I haven't officially met with or personally spoken to the plug as of yet..."

"I'm confused."

"Put it like this, I was in a restaurant down Fells Point when I ran into Vanessa. You know how I do, shinning, looking good. I guess Vanessa was feeling my swag from a distance. She sent me a bottle, and I accepted.

Minutes later we started rapping real heavy; it was like love at first sight.

After six months of her watching how I move, Vanessa felt it was time for me to step my game up, so she put a word in for me to her folks in Miami. She does all the communication for now."

Bradshaw was a hustler's hustler, seeing or experiencing almost everything one could in the drug game. From what Irvin told him so far, he liked. A solid connect with this kind of work could really put them in power.

If he himself was going to take a penitentiary chance, it had to be worth it; however, the glitz of the future was dependent upon this simple test run and how fast they could get the bread back to the plug. "Let's make a good impression."

With that being said, Irvin pushed a kilo in front of Bradshaw and said, "That's yours."

Stunned, Bradshaw asked, "What you want for this?"

Irvin felt a little insulted. "Get yourself right. I don't want shit back."

Bradshaw gave a wholehearted dap. "Good looking."

"That's what homeboys do."

Looking down at the brick, reality resonated. Not being home for a full month as of yet and he was back to getting his hands dirty. Measuring the situation for what it was, he knew the risk. But it was loyalty and fear of poverty that drove him to this point, which was now a decision he was prepared to live with. Bradshaw and Irvin stayed up the rest of the night cooking and bagging up coke.

$ $ $ $

At work the next day, book bag stuffed with rocks, Bradshaw set his personal plan into motion. For obvious reasons, he desired to move discreetly. Choosing to only serve his coworkers for the time being, Isaiah was the last person Bradshaw wanted to catch wind of his affairs. Buckling under the weight of his former lifestyle didn't make Bradshaw feel dignified; in fact, it was the total opposite. These hidden emotions became apparent the moment he pulled Weasel to the side in the locker room. Bradshaw hesitated when he said, "Yo, I...got some butters on the market."

Weasel's eyes lit up like Christmas lights. "Talk to me. What chu got?"

Bradshaw whispered, "Big twenties."

Clearly interested, Weasel parted his chapped lips and asked, "Give me one on the arm so I can see what chu working wit."

Bradshaw played fair and slid him one with no problem. "Don't have nobody in my business. If they want something, make them come to you, and you report to me. Keep it on the low."

Weasel's eyes glazed over as he gawked at the huge boulder in the plastic baggie. Indeed, he was anxious to sample the drugs. "Don't worry, negro. I know the game."

Never shocked by the antics of a crackhead, Bradshaw watched as Weasel made a beeline towards the restroom. Five minutes flew before the man emerged, sweating profusely, eyes bulging as if he'd seen a ghost. Bradshaw knew Weasel was beamed up but still asked, "How was it?"

Weasel did a geeky dance, pecking like a chicken with his neck. "I'm high as a fly. Negro, I ain't have no bomb like this in years."

After stretching the coke to its limit and it still pack a strong punch, Bradshaw knew the plug was official. They could make a lot of cash off such a pure product. Weasel's reaction had him convinced. "Snap out of it. Don't forget what I told you."

"I won't," said Weasel, immediately buying five more. "Oh, by the way, credit is a good thing around this piece. The check cashing place is next door, so you'll never have a problem with collecting your scrilla. Just food for thought."

The trash truck smashed the horn for them to come outside.

"I'll think about it, but let's get to work before they start without us."

Weasel pocketed the rocks and straightened out his hat. The two men then rushed out as if all was normal.

By time the shift drew to a close, Manny-El was in Bradshaw's bushes, using Weasel as a messenger to send the hustler to his office trailer.

Bradshaw was a little confused as to why his presence was demanded. All he could fancy was that Manny-El must knew he had some work by studying Weasel's odd behavior on the job. Bradshaw tapped on the door.

A gruff voice bellowed, "Come on in, buddy friend."

Enthused by his supervisor's chummy attitude, Bradshaw tried not to appear so skeptical as he entered. Inside of the office was bland, cloudy from cheap cigar smoke. Bradshaw registered the environment through squinted lids. "What's up?"

Manny-El was behind a hand-me-down desk. Forcing a big smile on his pock-marked face, natural oily skin made him look like a straight grease monkey. "I heard you had some drop?"

Though astounded at how fast word spread, Bradshaw realized Weasel just couldn't hold water. Now that the information was out, he kept it real.

"People like it."

Manny-El cut straight to the chase. "Give me a tester."

Bradshaw knew a shakedown when he saw one, but it was in his own best interest to appease his supervisor. He took out a twenty and pitched it upon the table.

As swift as a seagull snatches food out of the air when tossed, Manny-El scooped up the crack and retrieved a glass pipe.

Making short work of the rock right there on the spot, the high instantly clubbed him. "I definitely love it."

"Thought you would," uttered Bradshaw, snickering.

Manny-El took out two hundred dollar bills and waved them like half- staffed flags. "Can I grab fifteen of those for this? Look out for me."

It was a hundred dollar short, though new clientele was better than none. Bradshaw decided to grant him the deal. "Got chu this time, but don't make it a habit."

Manny-El stood up and shook Bradshaw's hand as if he'd just finished an interview. "Trust me...I won't."

Six more hundred was made before Bradshaw reached the exit gate. And there, as always, he ran straight into the big boss. He attempted to quickly pass the man to avoid small talk.

Isaiah pushed up on him. "So you're back in the fast lane again?"

Bradshaw stopped in place, unable to conjure a legitimate response, lips sealed.

Isaiah used the silence to his advantage. "If you keep doing what you did, you'll continue to get what you always got. The game isn't designed to produce winners. All it takes is one fumble for you to end up right back in the can."

Bradshaw had no choice but to justify his wrong doing. Zipped lips went out the window. "I ain't in it like I used to be. I'm just on some hit-and- miss shit."

"That's what they all say until calamity strikes. I thought you were stronger than that," berated Isaiah.

His words bit into Bradshaw. "Nobody's perfect. This country was built on crime. It's not like I'm putting myself on Front Street.

I know how to stay under the radar and not be reckless. Slow and steady wins the race. I refuse to let the system scare me into starvation."

Seeing the determination in Bradshaw, Isaiah switched the beat of his lecture. "All I'm saying is that you got to be smart, move with precision, take it to the next level. Find a legal venture to tie your money into. Don't be like the rest of them petty hustlers who grind with nothing to show for it. A true hustler could sell milk to a cow, so don't restrict your grind to just drugs."

Bradshaw let Isaiah's point of view marinate. It made sense. "You act like you know something about these streets."

Isaiah put on a wise smirk. "I did my tour out there, had thirty years of my life stolen by hard jail time. Don't be like me."

He was done listening to Isaiah preach. "I'm not going back to jail."

"I hope not."

Bradshaw concluded their conversation by abruptly walking off.

$ $ $ $

Drifting away in concentrated thought on his way home, Bradshaw contemplated what Isaiah told him. His boss made perfect points. Staying low key would be in his best interest. Besides building a reliable clientele at the job, Bradshaw only planned on dealing with those he knew, though he had to still cover his own safety from all angles. For that reason among others, he decided to cop a communication device. With that in mind, Bradshaw made a small detour.

A short ride later, he parked behind the historic Old Town Mall. The lot was empty. A few minutes to six meant most stores within the shopping strip were closed, which was a blessing because he always hated to pop up at public places alone or without a weapon. It would be his misfortune to run into a foe and be caught down bad. Being back into the life, though Bradshaw dreaded the idea while on parole, he had to consider totting a burner in the future. But for now he would creep in and out of Old Town Mall without being noticed.

As Bradshaw moseyed pass a small shoe store, he couldn't believe who he saw getting fitted for a pair of leather heels. It was his parole officer. Refusing to squander this chance opportunity, he snuck up on the woman unannounced, stealing her attention. "How are you doing, Ms. Rice?"

It took a fraction of a second to gain recognition. "Hello, Mr. Peatican. I'm fine. How about you?"

"Maintaining."

Feeling awkward, she probed, "What brings you to a ladies shoe store?"

He saddled a bold lie. "I came to pick up something nice for—"

"Your girlfriend?" A twinkle toured her eyes, lasting only a wink.

"Don't have one of those." He exercised calmness to make his lie fair seeming. "It's for my mother."

"How nice." She left it at that. "Is your transition coming along smooth?"

He blinked slow to emphasize a problem that didn't really exist. "It could be better..."

Spring gave chase. "In what way?"

"If I had the right woman by my side there's a chance I'd be more at peace."

To keep him mentally off balance, she curtly switched the topic by saying, "That's right, I have to set a home visit for you next week."

Bradshaw muttered, "Oh, I forgot to tell y'all I moved."

Her face crinkled in disappointment. "I could violate you right this minute."

He played naive. "For what?"

"You must notify me before you change addresses."

"My fault."

She rummaged through a handbag until locating a digital organizer. "What is the address?"

Bradshaw watched her punch the new information in as he dictated.

The parole officer explained, "You're lucky you bumped into me prior to my supervisor, Mr. Bart, conducting his follow-up. Now I'll be able to change it before he does. Who are you staying with?"

Relieved to have his mistake corrected, he let out a deep breath. "My homeboy."

She reiterated the importance concerning his terms of parole. "You may be physically free, but you're still the property of D.O.C. That means I must always know your whereabouts, so you shouldn't make any move without consulting me first. Like I said, you are lucky we crossed paths today."

Swallowed by her kindness, Bradshaw looked his P.O. in the eyes, "I don't believe in luck, only destiny."

Flustered, she broke eye contact.

Sensing the possibility of her being attracted to him, he hopped on her line. "Can I ask you a question off the record?"

By her standard, his request bore the likeness of a command. "These personal questions are becoming a pattern. Make it snappy."

He struck like a thunderbolt. "Where would you like to go when I take you out?"

His charm seemed sincere enough to sway her, "So...you just know we're going out, huh?"

Bradshaw seasoned his response with a comely smile. "I think you're feeling me the way I'm feeling you. If that's true, the next logical step would be us getting to know each other in a personal, friendly setting."

His confidence turned her on. "I won't say yay or nay. Let me think on Now that she was inside her own head, progress was being made. Bradshaw backed off, concluding, "Well, I hope your decision will be in my favor."

Spring kept it as professional as she could. "We'll see."

$ $ $ $

On Grub's usual day to get a cut, he strutted inside the shop to find Jake already gone. Willie D was enjoying a slice of pizza by the shampoo bowl when the angry man approached. "Where the fuck is Jake at?"

"No idea," answered Willie D with a full mouth.

Tim-Tim walked up on the conversation, sticking his nose straight in. "The nigga was just here ten minutes ago."

Grub's response came in a grunt, "That coon knows my routine. He never jetted like this before. What the fuck kind'a game he playing."

Tim-Tim gave Jake the benefit of the doubt. "Something important may've come up."

Between bites, Willie D added wood to his bosses flame, words escaping in a faint whisper, "I feel he on some brand-new shit, been on it ever since Bradshaw hit the bricks."

That gave Grub something to think about. He already found Bradshaw in Jake's chair twice, once even occupying his own seat, all of which were odd considering he'd been getting his haircut at the same time of the week, by the same person, for the last five years. Now it did seem like Jake was switching up, and Grub hated it. He said to Tim-Tim and Willie D, "I'll deal with that cocksucker on my time. But for the time being, keep an eye on him to make sure no hanky-panky is going on."

Both men took heed.

CHAPTER 5

A full month had past since Bradshaw begun hustling.

The job proved to be very lucrative on the positive and negative side. He was able to earn two grand a week, saving every dime for a rainy day. With only a few ounces sold, he still had a lot of work untouched. The product wasn't moving fast, but it was moving discreetly, and that was the only thing he was concerned with. To keep the police from chipping him over a petty matter, Bradshaw renewed his driver's license. With that accomplished, he felt more comfortable traveling with Doobie on their Friday outings. He actually felt safe and content with the way life was going.

On this particular Friday, Bradshaw was stepping out of the shower when the house phone rung.

Irvin answered, calling out, "Brad, come grab the jack."

Being it was payday, Bradshaw figured it was Peaches checking on him to see what time he'd be there to pick up Doobie. He wrapped himself in a towel and took the call. ""Wha'd up?"

"Hello, Mr. Peatican. This is Ms. Rice."

The voice pleasantly surprised Bradshaw, making his heart pound. She hadn't taken him up on his offer as of yet; in fact, the last few times he visited the parole office she implored him to refrain from asking personal questions, leading him to conclude that she had no interest at all. So even he started playing hardball.

"How can I help you?"

She giggled, adding extra sugar to her voice. "You sound like a robot.

It ain't that serious."

He spoke fast, "I'm off work, and the parole office closed. This my down time. If this a business call, call me during business hours."

She completely understood his frustration. "Be nice. This call isn't business, it's pleasure."

That made him listen up, "Oh, yeah. I heard that."

"I thought about your offer; the answer is yes, but don't make me regret this."

She just coated Bradshaw's day with strawberry icing, making him instantly shed his defensive attitude. "Now you speaking my language. This will not be a disappointment. I take it you made your mind up about where you want to go?"

"That depends on when you want to hang out."

"Tonight is good."

She didn't object. "Well, let's stick to something basic like a movie and dinner."

That was right up his alley. "I can live with that."

"We can meet some place, or I can pick you up. The choice is yours."

Remembering his prior engagement, Bradshaw explained, "I first got an activity to do with my son, but you can pick me up by nine."

Spring thought for a second. "Nine-thirty is better."

"Bet."

"I'll see you then."

Bradshaw was thrilled. "And I'll be waiting."

She chose not to say goodbye.

In preparation to look his best that night, the father promptly scooped up his son and squirted to the mall. On the way there, just as before, Doobie stuck his little nose in grown-folks business. "Dad, did you find a girlfriend yet?"

Assuming Peaches coached his son on what to ask in advance for nosey purposes, Bradshaw wasn't boggled at all by the spontaneous question. "Tell your mother to stop using you to piece together what I'm out here doing, okay?"

Doobie was intelligent enough to depict the obvious reason why his father made that statement. "No, she didn't told me to ask you that. I wanted to know for myself because I never seen you with another girl. What about the birds and the bees?"

He completely understood Doobie's concern of not wanting to see him alone, but it was best that his son stayed in a child's place. "The birds and the bees can wait. I don't want you worried about me in that way. Your dad can take care of himself. Like I told you not to worry about a girlfriend and focus on them school books, I feed myself the same advice. You don't have to chase girls. Right now my brain is screwed into work, making bread to build a good future for you and I. That's the only place my head is at, you get me?"

Not qualified to attest his dad's view, he shook his head up and down.

"Seriously, I'm good, kiddo."

Secretly wishing his parents were one, Doobie fell into silence with a quarter smile. It wasn't much he could do about the matter.

After going crazy in a pricey clothing store, their outing was over earlier than usual. Doobie was dropped off sometime around 8:30 p.m.

Rushing to the condo to get fresh, Bradshaw threw on a designer-jean set, a knitted sweater and a pair of motorcycle boots. When he told Irvin and Vanessa about his date, they were so intrigued over him booking his P.O., the couple cleared house, allotting the playa space to shine.

The doorbell rung 9:30 on the whistle. Like a pirate spotting treasure through a telescope, Bradshaw peered into the peephole and was pumped to see Ms. Rice on the other side. He opened the door and was captivated by her splendor. Revealing a perfect figure, she sported a red one-piece dress that hugged every curve between her neck and thighs. With her hair in thick curls, makeup flawless, and leather heels on the money, she wore a matching gold necklace and watch that shimmered almost as bright as her eyes. Her glow placed him at a loss for words.

She also marveled over how handsome he looked, saying, "Sharp...I like that."

Once Bradshaw picked his jaw off the floor, he reciprocated, "You look beautiful, Ms. Rice."

She tittered. "Thank you. And since this is an informal meeting, please, I insist you call me Spring."

Bradshaw now knew her on first name basis. His voice cracked as if dehydration was the cause. "That's what's up. Okay then, Spring, let's paint the town."

Amused by his enthusiasm, she responded, "Yeah, and have some fun.

Bradshaw followed her to a purple Porsche. The vehicle was definitely out the reach of her salary cap. Either she was a monster on the budget tip or had some big dough stashed in the bank. No matter how one conceptualized it, her ride was a beast, making Bradshaw feel like money when he sunk into the soft leather of the passenger seat. "This is a mean toy for a parole officer to have."

Spring hushed him with a measly wave of the hand. "This is nothing.

When you work hard, you play hard. I don't believe in cheating self. You only live once."

Bradshaw was impressed by her nonchalant disposition. It was more to Spring than what met the eye. Before he could comment on her philosophy, she shuffled the topic.

"I was thinking about catching Titanic; it's a movie that just came out."

That flick was great taste. "A few dudes at my job said it was like dat.

I wouldn't mind seeing it."

She glanced at the clock on the dash. "The next show time is at ten. Do you think we can make it?"

"In a car like this," Bradshaw reclined his seat, "I don't see why not. Do your thing."

The tires skidded.

Seconds into their commute, he used the in-between time to get to know her better. "Where you from?"

Spring kept her focus on the road. "East Baltimore."

Her answer was vague. Maybe he had to be more specific. "How about this, what school you went to?"

Spring's cheeks were caught some place between a smile and a frown.

"I graduated from Dunbar."

Bradshaw was stunned because that was the same school he flunked.

"What year did you graduate?"

In thought, her eyes rolled west. "Around the mid-eighties."

A gong sounded off in his head. "That's crazy 'cause I also went to Dunbar, dropped out in the tenth grade."

Spring was about to blow his mind, saying, "Boy, we went to school together as kids. Mr. Woods was your seventh-grade teacher. When you was in his class, I was in the sixth grade, Ms. Ashe's."

Recognition finally registered in a few slow blinks. "Oh, shit, I remember you; in fact, you was that little girl who always wore the long pigtails."

Spring knew she probably went unnoticed back then, as with many other unfortunate teens, due to having a flat chest and no fanny. "I blame those pigtails on my mother. She prepared me for school up until I got out of her house."

Bradshaw's memory became crystal clear. "Peaches and Shavon were your classmates."

"And that dude Calvin was yours. You and that boy rolled tough, couldn't see one without the other."

"Yeah," he spared her any up-to-date details, "it's a small ass world.

So you must be a year younger than me, twenty-six?"

"Yup," she smiled in agreement, "you hit it right on the mark."

Bradshaw scratched his head. "You look completely different from school. Why you ain't tell me who you was off the break?"

"You paid me no attention then, so why should I have thrown myself out there like that. Completely unladylike."

Which was a true bill in every sense of reality. Bradshaw ate that like a champ, taking it for what it was. As popular as he and Grub were in school, he considered the strong possibility, nine times out of ten, Spring had a crush on him way back when. "So, did you know who I was when you got my case?"

Spring didn't tell him that she personally requested his file. "I'll let you answer that for yourself."

With that information knocking Bradshaw out of the ballpark, his eyes shot spears through the windshield. "This is so weird."

The pair continued to catch up on old times until reaching the Harbor Park Movie Theater.

The flick lived up to its good rating. Bradshaw and Spring shared laughs, even drew close during some heart-wrenching parts of the movie. As soon as it was over, they sauntered by foot to a classy restaurant located on Pratt Street. The woman already had a table on reserve. Though Bradshaw begged to pay the full tab of their date, Spring insisted on treating him. He figured she knew what he made and didn't want to burn his little pennies on one night out. The pleasant gesture was sincerely accepted and left at that.

Seconds after the order was placed, Spring asked, "So, tell me, how do you utilize your free time?"

Bradshaw gave a half-truth. "I be looking into different business ventures, trying to get some legal money while staying clear of old associates."

She smirked. "You don't have to tiptoe around your words with me. Be real."

"I am," petitioned Bradshaw. "I'm on some new shit out here. Prison ain't for me."

Spring scoured his eyes for sincerity. Once satisfied, she added, "That's what I wanted to hear. Stay patient and opportunity will present itself. That's how the universe works."

"I definitely feel that. Believe me... I'm on my game."

For some unknown reason, Spring began to swim in his eyes.

He sucked at reading her thoughts. "Why you looking at me like that?"

She balanced her next question on a slippery slope. "What made you pursue me?"

Bradshaw spoke from the heart, "Besides me being a go-getter, your energy gravitated me towards you. I honestly wanted to see if we were compatible."

She was gratified by his answer. "I am completely attracted to your boldness. You are a strong man, and I believe strength should always be rewarded."

"You're my reward—"

"No," she strayed away from the truth, "this date is."

He refused to buy into her statement. "I like that curveball you threw."

Spring eyed him lustfully. "You're the one holding the bat."

Just when their conversation was about to get juicy, the sultry pair were interrupted by Grub, Tim-Tim and Willie D. The trio were decked out from head to toe, platinum everywhere.

Grub was cordial. "What's up, Brad. Didn't think I'd run into you here."

Shocked for a second, Bradshaw met him with a harsh look. "Ain't shit, doing what I do."

Even Grub recognized Spring off top but played the fifty. He intrusively asked, "Aren't you gonna introduce us to your lady-friend?"

"Yo," Bradshaw spoke with attitude, "you fuckin' up my groove. Catch me some other time."

A fatter face wasn't enough to omit childhood features. Though Spring knew exactly who Calvin was, she stayed silent, examining he and Bradshaw's interaction.

Grub caught the vibe. "You got that, playboy. I get up witchu on a later date."

Bradshaw stood firm. "Appreciate it."

Spring fixedly watched the three guys stroll off. She could tell Bradshaw was upset. The concerned woman offered comfort by asking, "Are you okay?"

He found it difficult to preserve a humble demeanor. "I'm ready to bounce."

Just to dead the negative energy, Spring concurred by clutching her purse. "Yeah, let's get out of here."

During their short walk to the car, Bradshaw apologized. "I'm sorry for ruining our night."

"It's fine," responded Spring.

Bradshaw filled her in on a little history. "That fat dude was Calvin; he goes by the name Grub now."

She didn't know that Calvin and Grub were one in the same. "You're doing the right thing by not associating with him. He's bad news."

Bradshaw shot her a curious gander as if she was already down with what he was about to disclose.

Spring exchanged a similar expression before saying, "I had no clue that Grub was Calvin's nickname. According to the streets, Grub is one of the biggest dealers in the city. Even the police stay out of his way. That's why I said what I said."

"Thanks for clearing that up." A second wave of anger washed in as Bradshaw continued to peel the scab of his past. "Well, anyway, we used to be partners in the drug game, that was before I caught my time. I hate that nigga with a passion."

Spring interjected, "I can tell, but what gave you such a distaste for him?"

While confiding in her, Bradshaw totally overlooked Springs status as a parole officer. "I took the drug beef they convicted me for, but that was his shit, and he didn't lift a finger to help me. Just on the strength of that, I cut his fat ass off."

Spring shared in his anguish. "Smart choice. You shouldn't befriend anyone with that type of cross in their blood. As a man who stand on principles, you'll get your turn to shit on those who pissed on you."

With the woman in support of his emotions, that alone made Bradshaw feel better. Enough talk about Grub, it was time to focus on her. "The end of our date went sour, but let me fix it by taking you out next week. My treat."

As admiration seeped into her heart, she accepted. "That would be an honor on my behalf, but you pick the spot next time."

Happy to be granted another date after such a disaster, Bradshaw looped his right arm around Spring as they entered the parking garage.

"Not a problem."

$ $ $ $

Bradshaw awoke on the recliner the following morning. The first thought that came to mind was Spring. The fact she declined when he went for a goodnight kiss only heightened his level of respect for her as a person. *He could use a strong female like Spring in his life.* As Bradshaw continued to daydream about the woman who he hoped would become his future love, Irvin walked from the kitchen in boxers.

He beamed at Bradshaw as if reading his mind. "Yo, I peeped your P.O. when she dropped you off last night. Shorty ah beast."

Bradshaw stretched and proudly agreed. "Yeah, shorty is a real keeper. She'll be making a home visit on Wednesday, so make sure everything is in order."

"Want for something else," responded Irvin. "But on a business note, how your bank coming along?"

He paused to crunch some numbers in his head. "It's coming."

Irvin seemed irritated with that answer. "I'm figuring it might be coming too slow. I been finished my weight and already sent the money."

Bradshaw squinted. "You said that to say what?"

"It's a lot of bread out there with our names on it, especially down Flag."

A feeling of rage came and went without any real justifiable cause; he stood. "Flag is a death trap. If you can recall, that's where I caught my case. I told you from the get-go, I'm playing the background. Slow and steady wins the race. Thought we was on the same page."

Irvin got frustrated with Bradshaw's philosophy. "We are, but it's time to turn that page to the next chapter. If I had done seven years for another nigga and that same shit-ball was rich when I touched down, I would'a wanted mine off top."

Bradshaw ate that. "Every thing takes time. I'm not just tryin' to get it,

I'm tryin' to get it smart. Even though parole got me by the balls, I'm still taking chances. When I said I had your back, that should have been enough."

Irvin gave him no cushion. "I feel all that, but 1 need you fully committed. Miami talking 'bout shooting fifty birds on consignment. I don't want to take up that huge responsibility unless you're in all the way...for the long haul."

Bradshaw read between the lines. "You already accepted the consignment, didn't you?"

Looking like he was caught between a rock and a hard place, Irvin sighed. "I did, but—"

Bradshaw huffed, eyes darting at his little homie. "Why would you do that without consulting with me first?"

Irvin gave a reminder. "I already told you about the connect and getting better work for the low."

"You mentioned nothing about consignment. That game is played by different rules. And fifty birds is a lot of work. You should have put me on point before you made this commitment. I would have been prepared."

The boy's words flowed much softer then intended, "I made the deal so it could put us on top. If I unload that type of work in the hood, Grub would put a hit on me, but he scared of you. Now if you stamp it with your name, he won't say shit."

Bradshaw hummed wordlessly. It had to be a better way to dispense the work without throwing himself under the bus. "I don't want them alphabet boys on my ass. It's a thousand ways this can go wrong."

Irvin exercised optimism. "It'll go good as long as we use the right strategy. The connect wants back five hundred thousand. You and I can split the rest down the middle. Start your own business with your share, be out the game just as fast as you jumped in. Plus, I got a squad of dudes from the projects who ready to get money. Give me the word, and it's on."

After wiping beads of sweat from the bridge of his nose, Bradshaw asked, "How long do I have to think?"

"The work will be at the Port on Monday."

Completely indecisive, Bradshaw lightly hammered his fist against the wall.

Irvin was willing to do or say anything to get him totally on board. "Bro, we'll move however you see fit. You can be the Captain of this Mayflower. Everything can move according to your plan, promise."

Bradshaw realized his little buddy was trying to hand the authority and brains of the operation over to him. With the magnitude of this giant responsibility on his shoulders, Bradshaw's head had to be in the game. As long as he himself was in charge, he could create a format that best suited his own well-being. Keeping that in mind, Bradshaw leaped out there to help a friend. "For now, we'll keep buying from Grub to keep him at bay; therefore, he'll think it's his drugs you're selling. That will keep him out of your way for awhile."

Irvin first grimaced at the thought, that was until the genius of the idea crystallized. "Smart plan."

"And round up the soldiers. Tell them to meet us at Federal Hill by eight tonight. I need to get a feel of them."

Gassed up, Irvin gave Bradshaw a bro-hug. "For sure."

"Last but not least,' not a bone trembled in Bradshaw's body as he dictated his final request, "I need some heat in case shit get dirty."

Irvin chased their bro-hug with a heavy pound. "That's the nigga I know."

Still blown from being kept in the blind, Bradshaw muttered, "I bet."

Irvin rushed to the closet and grabbed a black duffle bag filled with weapons. "Pick what chu want."

"Goddamn," Bradshaw fumbled through all the guns, "you got a whole arsenal in here. These joints clean?"

Irvin shrugged. "Yeah, no, maybe so. I got an AR-15 and Street Sweeper in the back, too."

Bradshaw cuffed a Glock 23 and a MAC 10. "Both of these are definitely my style."

Irvin could see the old Brad coming into play. If his eyes served him right, the streets were now in trouble!

CHAPTER 6

Kia gave her brother a surprise call, insisting they meet for brunch. So thrilled to accompany his little sister, Bradshaw sped downtown as fast as he could. Now he was sitting across from her in the Cheesecake Factory. In cherishing this special moment with each other, the duo caught up on current events.

Kia was exceptionally talkative. "I'll be graduating from Law School in a couple weeks. I hope you'll be there."

At the end of swallowing down a strawberry pancake, he assured, "Wouldn't miss it for the world."

Kia barely touched her meal.

Her true purpose for hooking up with Bradshaw was to reconcile the relationship between him and her fiancé. "I know you don't like me with Calvin. You have a right to be mad at him, but you're so much bigger than that. Me loving him should mean something to you."

Wanting to appease his beloved sister, Bradshaw explained, "It does, but you have no idea all the shit I been through at the cost of keeping my mouth shut. For you not to hold me down, that shit hurts."

She hit him with the puppy-dog eyes. "I can't see myself marrying Calvin without your blessing. Please, please forgive him... for me."

Grub had Kia completely love struck and blind. If the nigga could cross him after all they'd been through, he was definitely capable of crossing her; however, that was a lesson Kia had to learn on her own. Until then, Bradshaw didn't want to ruin her happiness. "As much as it disgusts me to see y'all together, let-alone forgiving him for shittin' on me, I'll let it go for the sake of my love for you."

She pouted. "You meeean it?"

"Yeah," Bradshaw's toes curled in his sneakers, "consider it my engagement gift."

Overjoyed, she swatted his arm. "Oh, I just love you. Thank you, bro.

This means so much to me."

$ $ $ $

While watching Kia safely pull off after their bruncheon, Spring hit his phone. He let the call go to voicemail just to make it seem

106

like he was busy. A few minutes boogied before he returned a buzz. "Hey, sorry I missed your call, but I was in the middle of a business meeting. What's up?"

Sounding innocent, Spring responded, "I didn't want to disturb you.

I'm calling to say you could skip your regular Monday appointment this week, being that I will be conducting a home visit on Wednesday."

Her kindness was no puzzle to sort out; she was simply cutting him a small break. "Lovely."

Nosy as the average female, Spring asked, "Did your meeting at least go well?"

Wanting to impress her, he answered, "In fact, it actually did."

"Great."

"The way it looks, don't want to speak too fast, some investors may be helping start up my own business."

Spring probed. "What kind of business?"

A lie floated off his tongue. "I'm trying to buy a barbershop around my old way. It's on the market, so I thought I'd take advantage of it."

She wished him well. "I hope everything works out for you. But parole wise, if this venture becomes your source of income, you must have definite proof, all paperwork intact."

Bradshaw was already sharp. "I know."

She prompted his ambition. "I like to hear positive things. Keep up the good work. I'm in your corner if you need me."

He kept his emotions unreadable. "That's nice to hear."

Spring also played mental chess. "Well, I guess, I should be going."

It pained Bradshaw to hang up. If he could, he would have kept her on the phone for the remainder of the day. "Can I call you later?"

Spring warmly replied, "You can use my number whenever you want."

That brightened his spirits. "Works for me."

"Talk to you soon."

Bradshaw was elated when the call ended. He almost wanted to kiss the phone. Chatting with Spring was intoxicating, but he had to put his head back on the real meeting scheduled for tonight.

By the time the sky struck a dark tint, Bradshaw was making his way up the sidesteps of the historic Federal Hill. The landmass was a spacious park directly behind the Inner Harbor. It exhibited antique statues and cannons as relics of the Civil War. Pet lovers used the park to walk dogs; families used it for parties and picnics; couples used it to relish the priceless view from its towering hill. Bradshaw had no interest in none of the above attractions. He was only there to examine the group of youngsters Irvin handpicked to help build their enterprise. Bradshaw had to damn-near tread the whole park before spotting the Lexus. As he approached Irvin and the crew, he recognized each boy as those who were always posted up inside his mother's building. The five were only kids when he went to prison.

Giving straight eye-contact, Bradshaw dapped them all. "What's hood?"

Keeping their poker face's intact, they responded in union with the body language of shrugged shoulders and head bobs.

Irvin introduced them one by one. He pointed to the first to step up.

The boy was 674" and almost 300 pounds. His black ass looked like he played professional football. At only eighteen years old, he was the most feared brawler down Flag House Projects.

"This is Ocky. He'll be our enforcer."

Ocky added emphasis by pounding his right fist into his left palm.

Standing beside Ocky was a fat kid in a multi-colored shirt, blue jeans and cream boots. Hanging around his neck was a dookie rope with a gold- cross medallion. Swirling waves consumed his dark Caesar.

Irvin pointed to him next. "This pretty motherfucker is Fred, but don't let the sweet taste fool you. He could sell a hook to a fish. Yo ah straight hustler."

Minus the baby face, Bradshaw said to himself that Fred would make the perfect front man. The boy had undeniable swag.

The third to step forward was a kid who weighed no more than a hundred pounds soaking wet. Not only did he have severe acne, but he was also missing an incisor. Irvin introduced him as Tabo.

"This pimple-faced nigga will be our point distributor. He's awesome with keeping money straight."

Bradshaw knew Tabo was one of those thugs who hugged the block; he had that look about himself.

Ed stepped up after Tabo. At just fifteen years of age, he had the strong features of a grown man. Rocking a nappy bush wrapped in a bandanna, long T-shirt and run-down Timb's, Ed was a killer who cared less about his outdoor appearance. He had a serious demeanor that signified danger.

Irvin tagged him in by saying, "I know you remember Ed from messing with his sister, Shavon. He's not that same snotty-nose little nigga begging for quarters. Baby boy plays with that pistol."

Bradshaw definitely recalled Ed's younger years when Shavon would trick him with cookies and candy to leave the room so they could fuck. Looking at Ed made Bradshaw momentarily envision his sister.

The last and elder of the mob was Sparky. He and Irvin were both twenty-three. Also, just like Irvin, the Latino looking fella had dark, curly hair and a light complexion. Sparky naturally stood out as a leader. Before Irvin could say anything about Sparky, Bradshaw already felt it best to make him lieutenant of the crew.

"Sparky's street credibility speaks for itself," said Irvin to Bradshaw. "The hood loves that nigga. We'll put him in charge of all day-to-day operations. That's my suggestion, but you're the boss. You call the shots."

Bradshaw skipped the formality of introducing himself. The Projects knew his work. He was labeled as a gangster in the hood. Bradshaw let Irvin's recommendations ride only because he trusted his judgment. His focus was on the crew. "I have y'all here to discuss business. I got a lot of work coming in and need some solid niggas to pump it. I'm paying two grand a week until the first shipment is done. After that, your base salary will jump to five thousand."

Fred spoke for the rest. "Damn, that's love, but how long do we have to move the shipment?"

Irvin chimed in, "One month."

Bradshaw looked at Sparky. "The product is going in fat jugs, that's to kill competition. How much do you think we can pull a day?"

Sparky went into his head to guesstimate. "We could probably move two bricks a day."

Tabo gave his take on the numbers. "I say four, if we run an overnight shift."

Bradshaw scratched his chin, inadvertently exposing a lack of knowledge. "That make sense, but the corners might get too hot to run a twenty-four hour shift."

Everyone stared at each other in a weird way.

Though he hated to do it in front the squad, Irvin caught the vibe and put Bradshaw up on game. "My nigga, you been locked down without the scoop. Dudes don't hustle on the corners no more, they use the steps in the buildings."

Now Bradshaw was the one confused.

Irvin continued, "Check it out, we first find a good stash house in the building to make our headquarters, arm the team with guns, then open shop on the third or fourth floor. That way we'll be out of sight. The fiends wouldn't want to get blown away, so they know to make some noise when walking up the steps. Once they reach the squad, they'll tell them what they want, cop and go. We run it just like that all day, feel me?"

To Bradshaw, that explained why he seen all the activity going in and out of the buildings. Niggas was operating a whole different way of hustling then when he was home. But he had to ask, "What about the police?"

Ed broke that part down, "You put a fiend on the front door and one in the back, play area as look-outs. If either see a police close to the building, they'll yell a code name so everybody inside the steps can run to the stash house. The fiends will let us know when it's clear, then we'll come back out to continue shop."

"That's tec," said Bradshaw, turning back to Irvin. "But I'm not trying to open shop in the 107 Building. Never shit where your family live."

Irvin felt Bradshaw had a frivolous gripe. "Grub already runs shop out of the 107 and 126 Building; he got those two on lock. But the 127 Building is up for grabs. Nobody hustles there only because the police's sub-station is right next to it. We can bust the steps in that building wide open."

Bradshaw thought for a second. "Sounds pretty risky."

"Hustling drugs is risky, period," stated Fred.

Ocky put in his two cents. "We could use a spider team, that's two pairs of fiends instead of one. Can't go wrong with eight eyes."

Bradshaw did enjoy how everybody were putting their heads together to make it work. "It all sounds wonderful, but once this

113

pure product hits the market, nobody will make a dime instead of us. That's when hating begins, niggas want to shoot at you and call the police. With this plan, we can't be caught slipping."

Fred voiced a serious concern, "How do you think Grub will respond once our shop starts booming?"

Bradshaw straightened the record, "Grub is really a cold bitch. Yo not gone want smoke. He knows how I get down, so don't worry about that. It'! solve itself."

"Fuck all the talking," said Irvin. "Let's get this money. Is everybody wit it or not?"

The team verbally committed themselves and was ready to roll with the punches.

Bradshaw concluded the meeting with, "I need y'all to trust my judgment. As long as y'all keep it gangster and stay loyal to the cause, we gone eat. That's my word."

All present dapped with satisfaction. The most important part of the plan was now in motion.

$ $ $ $

On a rough Park Heights block known for mayhem, murder and its open-air drug market, Yella and his right-hand man stood in the trenches.

While sharing a blunt, Yella said, "Dog, it can't get no better than this. We got the money, power and respect. What else could you ask for?"

Tyson took hold of the blunt, his pie face and flat nose almost making him appear as an ugly Martian through thick smoke. "I can't think of one thing. Maybe a jet or some shit."

Yella jokingly mustered, "Or maybe we should get two giant statues of us made and set them bitches right in the middle of the hood."

Tyson handed the blunt back. "I appreciate the gesture, but our success is all you. The hood stands on your name alone. You're so real it's unreal. Sho' nuff, niggas would die for you at the drop of a dime. Park Heights would be lost without your muscle and wisdom, that's on my dead mother."

"I feel that," responded Yella, "but I couldn't have risen this high without a nigga like you thuggin' by my side, ready for any and everything. I'm not too arrogant to admit that. You put in just as much work as me. So, as I climb up the ladder, you will too. Never would I leave my nigga behind."

"That's why I love the shit out of you," said Tyson, grabbing the blunt.

"That goes two ways."

"No doubt."

Yella fell back in a zone. "Now back to those two statues. What I was saying was..."

$ $ $ $

Before Bradshaw could blink, as always, Monday was already upon him. All day he'd been on pens and needles. As bad as he wanted to take off from work to assist his little partner, Irvin thought it best to make the pickup alone. The plan was for him to hit Bradshaw the moment he got the shit. And as if racing to the parole office on his usual Monday visit, Bradshaw would shoot home instead. Not having to be stuck inside of the parole office today, definitely while on standby at a time like this, was a blessing. In the middle of Bradshaw spreading the new word to his clientele at the trash spot, his device finally went off with Irvin's code on its screen.

$ $ $ $

Spring daydreamed about Bradshaw while on a computer at the office. Scratching his appointment without probable cause violated the established policy for high-risk parolees, but she was beginning to like Bradshaw too much to keep subjecting him to the scrutiny of her job's demands. How long Spring would be able to separate business from their personal relationship was a question unknown. While his mind was arrow-straight pertaining to being a productive, square citizen, which was beautiful in and of itself, that positive mentality hindered Spring from what she really had planned for him. Spring warned herself to give it time until the gravity of poverty fractured the levee of his defense mechanism, and only then would she introduce a business proposal that he couldn't resist. *This was her only reason for requesting his file from the beginning.*

As she clicked away at the keypad in frozen thought, Mr. Bart slithered like a serpent to the doorway of her office. The evil expression on his face was enough to frighten the average person. It seemed as if steam would shoot from his ears at any second. Spring spoke crutly, "Can I help you with something?"

No answer.

"Are you deaf...I'm talking to you."

Instead of falling into his usual hunt mode, Mr. Bart stood there with a fixed stare like a mannequin.

Spring got real uncomfortable. "Don't block my office door like some mute serial killer, SPEAK!"

Mr. Bart turned and walked off.

That was the chilling moment Spring knew her supervisor would potentially be a serious problem in the future.

$ \qquad $ \qquad $ \qquad $

Bradshaw sped home in anticipation of executing plan B. He walked through the condo's door to find Irvin pacing the living room. "What's the bizz?"

"You already know," responded Irvin, excited.

"Oh," Bradshaw let out an exhaustive breath, "I thought something was wrong."

"Naw, everything is right." Irvin grabbed Bradshaw and pulled him to the closet. "We got the work. The connect already had a delivery dude waiting on me at the Port. He tailed me and bought the shit straight here. It was easy."

Bradshaw was impressed by the connect's efficiency. He opened the closet door to fifty bricks of pure fishscale. Awestruck, the veteran hustler realized he'd never seen this much cocaine at once. The sight of it instantly explained why Irvin was so psyched. "It's unbelievable."

The young man put his arm around Bradshaw. "Did you and Grub have it like this when y'all was partners?"

"Fuck no!"

"Yo, I always wanted to be down with you, making money, running the projects. It's finally about to happen."

As Irvin got sentimental, for some reason Bradshaw's mind said this was the part of the movie where one greedy homeboy blast the other and skip with the work. Being he felt nothing of the sort forced him to recognize his genuine love for shorty. "You're more than a partner to Me. We're brothers. You had big do-right when I was in prison, then set me straight when I got out here. Nigga, you a dinosaur; they don't make'um like you no more. Whatever happens, good or bad, nothing will ever come between our bond."

Irvin had an unlimited supply of love and respect for his mentor. "You like a brother to me, too. I do right because you taught me the game. Broke or rich, it's us against the world."

Caught in the occasion, the two hugged each other like brothers of the same mother. Both were on the brink of some major power moves.

When Irvin parked in front of the 127 Building, the projects was crowded, buzzing with fiends. Strapped with pistols, Sparky and Ed met the pair. Totting a designer carrying bag, Bradshaw asked his appointed lieutenant, "Yall ready to kick this shit off?"

Sparky stepped close to his big man. "You fuckin' right. Everyone else is upstairs on standby."

With that discussed, the four took the steps to the fifth floor. The corner apartment was Lisa's dwelling. The slim, tight-eyed woman was a neighborhood crack whore, who was notorious for spitting in a cop's face. Bradshaw remembered how Lisa used to hang with his mother, both once being the sexiest women in the hood. Now they were neck-and-neck on the skeleton tip. Even their apartments had a slight resemblance. Roaches, trash and outdated furniture were to be expected of Lisa's pungent pad. Not one electrical appliance survived her daily crack binge. The place was in shambles.

The remaining crew members stood around in the kitchen, smoking weed and nursing beers. Everybody greeted Bradshaw and Irvin in a traditional hood manner.

Bradshaw informed the boys, "I'll drop the first package off tomorrow morning. It'll be some hammers with it as well."

Ocky felt proud to mention the team's progress, "We been spreading the word. The geekers are anticipating a bomb."

"Good," said Irvin. "That's why we brought y'all two ounces to chop down and give out as testers."

Bradshaw studied Lisa's dingy joint and made a mental note to personally speak with her. "This will be our headquarters. Tabo and Ocky, you two will run the day-shift, six to six. Ed and Fred will take the graveyard stretch. Sparky, you'll oversee both shifts, dropping in periodically to collect the bread. It's your responsibility to make sure the shop runs smoothly."

Fred commented, "We should pull another person to alternate through both shifts."

Ed jumped in, "What do you think Sparks here for, duuhhh. That grass and drink got you making stupid ass suggestions."

"And that's another thing," Bradshaw paused to give the crew an opportunity to open their minds, "don't get caught slipping out here. We got to stay one step ahead of all enemies and competition. Moving with precision means y'all got to keep the intoxicants to a minimum. Each of us have a job to do. Every individual is responsible to carry out his role."

The kitchen was quiet.

He continued, "I'm the boss of this team, which means I'm the face of the operation. If anything goes to shit, I'll take the brunt of the blow. It's my job to make sure all these other ballers, including Grub, respect our shop.

Things flowing with ease ensures that we're one step ahead of prison or mishaps. It can't be two bosses. If one of y'all got a problem with that, let me know so we can handle that shit right mutherfucking now..."

No one spoke up.

"Irvin is second in command. All problems will go to him first, and he'll be the one to translate those problems to me. Remember, unnecessary violence brings on heat. We can't afford that. What one does will affect the rest, so move smart. Hard work will be rewarded. Any form of laziness won't be tolerated. Questions?"

The crew had no inquiries. Enough was already said. Their facial expressions were that of motivation.

"That's right. I see the hunger in y'all eyes," grumbled Irvin. "Let's get this shit poppin'."

CHAPTER 7

Since Bradshaw was already down Flag, he took advantage of the opportunity to drop some cash on his mother. While at her apartment, she stressed concern over not seeing the twins in three days. Heading back to the 127 Building, it was perfect timing when Bradshaw ran into the frisky pair standing right beside the Lexus. "Ma looking for yall."

"Goddamn, Brad, what kind of police shit you on," jested Keema.

Irvin rolled up his windows to stay clear of their family dispute.

"Look," Bradshaw spoke with Keema as Kenya turned her back to him, "call me what you want. Y'all grown and I respect that, but don't be selfish to the ones who love you. I think you two should check in and let Mommy know y'all alright."

"We good," said Keema with the whole neck dance. "Me and my sister chasing this money. Since you moved out, Mommy been having a problem with us bringing boys home, so we do what we do out here, just so we don't have to hear her mouth."

Bradshaw stepped to Keema. "But y'all will hear mine because that shit ain't right. You two are going about things wrong."

Kenya sucked her teeth to agitate.

"Who you making them sassy noises at?" yelled Bradshaw, referring to the second twin.

"I'm not saying a word to you," uttered Kenya.

"So you still carrying a funky attitude towards me?"

Kenya sucked her teeth even louder.

Bradshaw converted into a mode of folly to match her immaturity. Without anymore rap, he leapt forward and swept her in a bear-hug. She fought for a second until he playfully bit her neck like a vampire.

"Sssstop," whined Kenya in a giggle.

Keema grabbed him from the back.

"Oh, now you hussies gone bank me." Bradshaw laughed and tussled until he was able to pin both twins against the Lexus. "See, y'all ain't strong enough yet."

"Oookay, ookay, okay." Keema submitted.

"You win," uttered Kenya, tapping out as well.

Bradshaw eased off of them. "I love y'all and don't want us to be at odds. I'm sorry for that little house incident. That's water under the bridge."

The twins were also apologetic, openly repenting for the roles they played in the past matter.

Bradshaw pulled a thousand dollars out of his pocket. "Here's a small something to keep y'all busy for a second."

That's when the hugs really poured in.

"Thank you," said Keema, snatching the bread.

Kenya was suspicious, asking questions that even his mother didn't impose. "This ain't no job money, You're back to hustling, aren't you?"

He didn't lie. "Something like that. I'm opening shop in this 127 Building."

Neither badgered him.

"Just make sure you be safe," said Keema.

Irvin honked the horn as though he was ready to bounce.

Bradshaw pecked his sisters on their foreheads and jumped into the Lexus. Irvin smashed the pedal to rev the engine, causing the wheels to skid once slammed into drive.

The twins waved as they peeled off, proud that their brother was about to fuck the streets up again. The king was back.

$ $ $ $

Fiends used to go crazy for straight white; now it was all about the ready-rock. Those five test-run kilos were already cooked up on arrival, but this time pure fishscale doled the responsibility of them playing chef. Possessing a mean whip game, Bradshaw was sure he could transform two birds into three, which would give them an extra twenty-five bricks. With those pretty numbers, they could bring in close to one million and a half just by jugging up an even five hundred dollars off each ounce. That would give them a four hundred fifty thousand dollar split after paying the connect.

Once at the condo, Bradshaw and Irvin went straight to the tables. Taking absolute precaution to avoid catching a dirty urine, Bradshaw slid on surgical gloves and measured out a brick of B12, which went into a huge pot on the stove, along with two kilos and a pitcher of water. As the liquid came to a boil, the white and cut began to fuse.

Irvin looked on studiously. He remembered when Grub used to refer to Bradshaw as a chemist for his prowess in stretching coke and dope.

"Damn, that shit is sticking good."

"Go get me a bowl of ice," prompted the crack doctor.

Like an eager apprentice, Irvin sped to the freezer.

Bradshaw spanked the work into a thick paste. Ten minutes later, putting his wrist into it, that same paste locked up. In went the ice cubes before it was removed with a large scooping utensil. He completed the process by using a microwave to absorb the remaining moisture. Once weighed, the work was a little over three thousand grams.

Placing several cases of empty jugs on the table, Irvin smiled at the results. "Yo, we "bout to crush these niggas."

Amazed his wrist game was still up to par, Bradshaw took the work off the scale. "Better them than us."

They stayed up late packing product.

Without any shut-eye, Bradshaw was out the door at 5:00 a.m. Since Irvin wasn't a morning person, he traveled alone to drop off the first book bag. Shockingly, Bradshaw was completely composed, far from nervous. In twenty minutes from his time of departure, he was standing in front of Lisa's apartment. After a few taps on the door, Lisa yanked it opened without even asking for his identity.

"Where them niggas at?" inquired Bradshaw, walking inside.

She spoke with arousal, "They bundled up in the room like a litter of puppies."

Annoyed, he called out to them, "Come on, y'all. It's work to be done."

Sparky shouted from the back, voice groggy, "Hold up...here we come."

Lisa smiled with stained teeth, "Boy, I ain't seen you in years."

"Yeah, I know, but I'm back out here like I never left."

She donated one of those hugs that a peasant would give a prince. "I know that's right."

Bradshaw put his mouth to her earlobe. "I need your eyes out here. Find four fiends, two each to watch the back and front of the building. Y'all will get paid a hundred dollars a day."

Not approving of a punk-ass hundred dollars, Lisa took a step back for clarity. "You mean to split?"

The nature of a crackhead was a trip. "Naw, ah'piece."

That sounded much better. "You know I'll do whatever you want, Brad."

"Report anything you see or hear."

Scratching her backside as if she forgot to wipe, Lisa reassured, "I got chu, boo."

Sparky pounced out of the room, tucking his shirt, rubbing the crackers from the corner of his eyes. "Big dog, what it is."

Ocky and Tabo slowly shadowed their lieutenant like two zombies.

Inwardly, feeling that sleep was the cousin of death, Bradshaw saved the boys from a lecture. He focused on Spanky. "Yo, here's the work. There's five guns in the bag as well. Irvin will grab the bread at the end of the shift. Stay on point."

While responding to his boss, Sparky elbowed Lisa out of the way. "I'll make sure everything is ready."

"Say no more." Bradshaw gave out pounds and dipped. Being so preoccupied with such an enormous task, it was weird how he heedlessly misplaced the though of Spring. A portrait of her face danced across his mind on the way to work.

$ $ $ $

Blowing the dust out of his Nintendo to make it work, Lunchbox fought against slamming the poor machine on the floor. It wasn't really the game console that had him hot, his true anger derived from Irvin not returning any of his buzzes since last week. How was he suppose to keep the geeker's attention without crack? Being dry for a few days contributed to Lunchbox spending most of his drug-bill money on highs and fun. In so many words, without a doubt or contradiction, Irvin was beat for the cash.

"Fuck dat nigga," grumbled Lunchbox. "He think he all that. Soon I won't need no one; I'll be the man, humph."

$ $ $ $

Work was work, nothing new. The only highlight of the evening was that the crew handled business with perfection. In fact, they almost sold out. Impressive for a debut. Bradshaw hit the sack as soon as he got to the condo, waking early on Wednesday to repeat the morning drop-off. Hooking work was a no-brainer since Spring would be conducting her home visit by ten.

Bradshaw used the spare time to shower and spiffy up the spot. In setting the mood, he ordered steak and red wine from a local caterer, arranging the table with lunch for two. Slow music played in the background. Irvin and Vanessa were no help, both sleeping through it all with the bedroom door shut. So long as they were out the way, that was sufficient enough for Bradshaw.

Spring arrived twenty minutes earlier than her scheduled appointment. Bradshaw immediately welcomed her inside, greeting the woman with a fresh rose.

Though in professional mode, she couldn't resist such a sweet gesture.

"Are you trying to seduce me?"

"Of course," he affirmed.

"Nice try for a man who forgot my number." She gave him the evil eye.

Bradshaw could see a hidden smile within her frown. "I take that charge. Please understand I been caught up trying to get on my feet out here. I didn't want to call you with a bunch of excuses as to what and why. Just know, you was thought about."

His excuse wasn't authentic, but it was acceptable.

"Let me find out you missed me..."

That made her blush. "Something like that."

"The feeling is mutual." Bradshaw kissed her hand. "Welcome to my home."

She appraised the condo, surveying the richness of good taste. "This is a beautiful place you have here."

"Thank you," responded Bradshaw, taking her coat and briefcase like a gentleman.

"Why does it feel like I've been lured into a spider's web?" remarked Spring.

"Because you have," answered Bradshaw, seating her at the table.

Skeptically, she inquired, "Where's your roommate?"

He poured them both a glass of wine. "Out for the morning."

She declined the alcoholic beverage. "I don't think that would be a good idea. I'm still on the clock."

Bradshaw removed the steak from its aluminum plan. "A few sips wouldn't kill you."

Being that he went to such great lengths to meet her pleasure, Spring gave in. The two ate and drank, chatting much about the past and of some things yet to come. As the wine took over, the tipsy woman came so close to telling him about her supervisor but refrained. That would've birthed more questions than she was willing to explain. Though leaving that urgent subject in limbo for now, Spring couldn't help but wear the emotional strain of it on her face.

Bradshaw immediately picked up on the shift. "What's wrong?"

Spring's inner confusion possessed the moment, causing her to look away. "Nothing."

Her body language led him to believe otherwise. "If there's something bothering you, talk to me. We can work it out together."

The correct buttons were indeed pushed, but Spring stuck to her guns.

Now wasn't the time to tackle it. "I'm okay, really."

Yearning to alter the negative energy, Bradshaw took her by the hand. "Would you care to dance?"

Spring loved the way he handled the situation. Without a fight, she leapt into his arms, swaying gracefully to the sound of Luther. They met eye contact while in the groove. Bradshaw initiated a kiss by sticking his tongue into her mouth. She sucked passionately. He furthered his advance by cuffing Spring's ass cheeks, working both hands up the small of her back. Down came the zipper to her blouse.

Before Bradshaw could hit a homerun, Irvin walked inside the kitchen, naked.

The kissing stopped.

"Oh, shit," said Irvin, embarrassed.

Spring was more humiliated than him. Speechless, she stood for a second in shock, then stared at Bradshaw as if being deceived. The vibe was destroyed. She broke free from his embrace.

Bradshaw unwittingly added more fuel to the fire by simply playing stupid. "Yo, I ain't know you was home."

"My bad." Irvin caught on, dashing from sight.

Bradshaw turned back to Spring, but it was too late. "That wasn't suppose to happen."

"But it did." Spring refastened her blouse. "Its time for me to get back to the office. You've passed your home inspection."

He reached for her. "Don't do me like that."

She knocked his hands away. "Stop it."

He pursued with more vigor.

"I said no!"

Her sternness threw Bradshaw completely off. "I didn't mean to make you feel uncomfortable. That wasn't my intention."

Spring retrieved her coat and briefcase, finding her own way out. "Mr. Peatican, your home visit is over. I'll see you at the office on Monday."

When Spring departed by slamming the door in his face, Bradshaw felt terrible within. Two disasters in a row was an ugly look, both bad timing. Neither was Irvin's fault. Bradshaw could only blame himself for being untruthful.

Unsure what to do next, he put the bottle of wine to his lips and killed the rest of it. Though it would have been beautiful, Bradshaw accepted he and Spring's personal relationship as a dead issue.

CHAPTER 8

After he and Irvin made light of the situation by laughing their asses off about it, they shot down the projects to monitor the shop. The 127 Building was banging with big traffic. The look-outs were vigilant and on point. The men took the elevator to the fourth floor and bopped across the ramp to hit the steps. Bradshaw observed the actual setup for the first time. Sparky was supervising with his revolver cocked, Tabo was posted with a machine gun and Ocky was sitting on a crate with a Footlocker bag filled with jugs. Not interrupting the team's routine, Bradshaw and Irvin stood as two flies on a wall.

"Make some goddamn noise!" shouted Ocky down the steps.

"Yo, yo, yo!" echoed a males voice from below. The middle-aged guy encountered the group of five.

"How many you need?" asked Ocky.

The guy tried to block out the fear of being mistakenly shot while copping his fix. "I'll take five."

Sparky took the fifty dollar bill, and Ocky handed the fiend five joints.

The fellow's eyes almost popped out of his face at the sight of how many large rocks were packed in each jug; they were the biggest he'd ever seen in the projects. He tipped his baseball cap with a smile and hopped back down the steps. Before he could make it to the first floor, a few more fiends were on their way up.

"Make some goddamn noise!" shouted Ocky.

Instead of a drive-thru, Bradshaw seen the shop as a walk-thru, for the short time he and Irvin spent there with the boys, the traffic stayed consistent. Each transaction was an in-and-out thing, a well oiled machine operating without flaw.

$ $ $ $

Spring couldn't think straight at the job. It wasn't that she felt played; moreover, it was a matter of disappointment. If Bradshaw could lie over something so frivolous, there was no way to trust him for what she had planned. Spring told herself that perhaps he was just thinking with his dick, willing to say anything to be with her. Or what if he really didn't know his roommate was still home? Did she overreact, jumping the gun without accepting his explanation. Considering the possibility of being at fault for having a closed mind, he deserved an apology.

Nonetheless, Spring fantasized over the softness of his lips, the heat of his tongue, both blew her away. She ached for more.

$ $ $ $

On their way to grab a bite before heading home, Irvin spoke with arrogance behind the wheel, "Once our feet get planted, we 'bout to take over Flag House. Since all this bread 'bout to flow our way, I say we should buy some fly rides just to shit on these niggas."

Bradshaw couldn't knock Irvin for feeling amped over spearheading a crack shop, but it was too early in the game to get big-headed. "Bro, we already gonna attract attention. Attracting the wrong kind, jackers and haters, will make us spend hell of energy protecting the shop. Once the bodies start falling, the police get involved. We got to avoid the heat."

As if he'd heard nothing, Irvin flipped his angle, modifying the same suggestion. "Yo, we can cop the new whips but not drive them to the hood."

"Maybe you need to clear out your ears," Bradshaw sternly muttered. "No matter if we drive them down there or not, we don't need to floss yet, period. There's plenty of time to do that. Building our paper is the key right now. It's best that we remain unseen, you feel me?"

Irvin piped down. "You right."

Bradshaw read the disappointment on the boys face. "We got to save and find some legitimate way to wash the cash. I know you're feeling yourself, but let the crew shine. We'll get the paper; everything stays balanced that way. This ain't a race...it's a marathon. Slow down."

That's not really what Irvin had in mind. He would rather them ball like boss-players, be internationally known as bubbling kingpins. But for the sake of needing Bradshaw's muscle, his inner thoughts remained unexposed. "Yeah," Irvin snickered, "make it look like the crew is eating better than us. In that way the spotlight would be on them."

Proud of his little homie's acuteness, Bradshaw gave him props. "You hit it right on the snout. Let the hood see them shine. All niggas want is cars, clothes, hoes, a solid reputation and street fame. They can have that. You and I will take the high road leading out the game. By the time shit hits the fan, like it always does, we'll be charged the fuck up. Selling crack will be a thing of the past."

"Pm wit it," responded Irvin, though not truly in harmony with the idea. He himself wanted to go down as a hood legend.

While they were rapping, Bradshaw's phone rung. Spring's phone number appeared, causing him to pop-lock in the passenger seat until regaining his cool. Trying not to shout for joy, Bradshaw told Irvin to stay quiet as he answered the call on speaker.

"What's up?"

Spring paused due to his animated tone. She couldn't determine if it was anger or excitement.

Not hearing anything on the other end made Bradshaw soften his voice. "Baby, say something. Are you there?"

Coming from him, Spring liked the way calling her baby sounded.

"Yes, I'm here?"

The sweetness of her voice instantly eased him. "You okay?"

She spoke as an innocent child, "I'm hitting you to say I'm sorry for the way I overreacted earlier. Your friend just caught me off guard."

Bradshaw elbowed Irvin on the pumped-up tip. "I bet he did.

Therefore, I should be the one apologizing—"

"Don't bother," she stopped Bradshaw, releasing him from self-pity. "I feel there's been too many apologies already exchanged between us. It clearly seems like we've been at the right places at the wrong times, never being afforded the privacy needed."

Just for the purpose of impressing Irvin, Bradshaw flexed an arm muscle like he was the man. "Yeah, I totally agree, but how do we fix it?"

"First we can start by having dinner at my place, but that's only if you accept my humble invitation."

Now the cat had Bradshaw's tongue. Even Irvin was shocked at her proposition.

Unsure if he'd hung-up, Spring whispered, "Hello. Did you hear what I said?"

Bradshaw finally got the knot out of his throat. "I did."

Spring got assertive. "So, is that a yes or no?"

Pleased with her show of trust, he responded, "A definite yes."

She gave him the address and giggled with satisfaction. "I'll be waiting."

"Not for long," he promised.

"See you then," Spring replied and hung up.

This was Bradshaw's third chance to make Spring his woman. The man was so hype, pumped out of his mind, he screamed at the top of his lungs, nearly blowing both of Irvin's ear drums. It seemed like everything was finally coming together in his life.

$ $ $ $

For the steps to only be on its second day of production, the gossip about it was already on swol. While smokers came by droves to get a fix, even street hustlers were copping several bundles at a time just to juggle.

Opinionated rumors bubbled that the steps were raking in over one hundred thousand dollars just on morning shift. Those numbers were astronomical compared to the other two buildings Grub was pumping out of. All of such was the lead topic inside the barbershop. Four of Grub's top dawgs huddled near Jake's station.

"Ever since the little niggas opened up on the steps, all the money been flowing to them. If this keeps up, a month from now the rest of Flag ah be down bad," said Tim-Tim to Willie D.

"Yeah, them clowns doing it big, but a limb don't cost a thing. That shit need to be shutdown," responded Willie D, giving his solution to the problem. "Tabo, Ed, Fred and Ocky can all come up missing."

"Who got them cranking?" asked Tim-Tim.

"They say Sparky the boss," uttered Yancy, quoting only what he heard from the streets.

"Them suckers must be holding some real work to stay on for twenty- four hours. That's big-boy shit," said Kavy with nothing but hate in his voice.

Tim-Tim had a hunch. "Do y'all think Irvin got something to do with it"

"If he does," Willie D thought with his eyes, "that's weight he got from our boss."

"Think," Tim-Tim poked Willie D in the side of his head, "he hasn't copped any weight from Grub in a minute. And even if he did grab a brick or two, Irvin wouldn't make any profit with them jugs so fat. It can't be yo."

"Fuck dat," said Yancy. "If they say Sparky the boss, that's who we should hit."

Kavy was with the drama, "I agree."

Tim-Tim took pride in solving problem's before it had a chance to reach Grub. He felt qualified to give the order. "Okay, we'll make him our target. If we happen to run across any of those other kids, they go too."

Jake was cleaning clippers at his barber station through the whispers of their whole conversation. Since Irvin's name came up, knowing that shorty was Bradshaw's little homeboy, Jake felt it only right to pass on the scoop he just heard.

$ \quad $ $ \quad $ $ \quad $ $

The sun was at its highest peak when Bradshaw hit the road. Since Spring's home was located in Bowie, Maryland he burned rubber in order to touch down at a reasonable time. The Fleetwood spun into the driveway before he knew it. Wearing a red robe and fluffy house slippers, Spring greeted Bradshaw with a wet kiss and gave him a tour of the mini-mansion. Even by the standard of a skilled interior decorator, the pad was plush from top to bottom, emblazoned with a feminine touch. The place had several bedrooms, three bathrooms, a den made for a queen, crystal chandeliers, deluxe model kitchen with state-of-the-art appliances, soft leather upholstery, two Jacuzzis, gigantic fireplace and a bar stocked with the best liquors.

Bradshaw was impressed by the time he reached her master bedroom. The floor and walls were made of marble. How she was able to afford such a classy joint was a bonified mystery. He attempted to fox her out. "Your spot is lik*dat. I didn't know parole officers made this kind of money for doing such an easy job."

Completely avoiding the discussion pertaining to her salary, Spring did add clearly to his false perception about the job being a piece of cake. "Working as a parole officer isn't as simple as you think."

Bradshaw eye-fucked Spring as she sat at a vanity beside tall veranda doors. "I mean...how hard could it be?"

"First and foremost, it's very exhausting. Only a heartless person would feel dignified separating men from their families. I didn't have a dad coming up, and that broke me. No child deserves to come up in a single or unstable household. With the judicial system and the streets assassinating black men to such an alarming degree, I would never gamble on having a child, especially raising it on my own. That's not for me."

Bradshaw was confused as to how a conversation about work switched to her not wanting a little one. Far from being in accordance with her bias theory on child bearing, he shielded his personal opinion by sticking to the original topic. "Well, it ain't like you're sending your own self to prison. I believe some people are really sick. Serial killers, rapists and child molesters need to be locked up or dead. There's no redeeming them."

She gave a contorted expression. "I do agree that some pencils come without an eraser, but the best treatment for hate is love. Most of my caseloads are good people who've been denied the right opportunities to reduce recidivism. Having a criminal history prevents them from obtaining certain employment, from living in certain crime-free neighborhoods and from being licensed for particular trades. But we order them to find jobs and stay out of the hood, though their options are limited. Parole is nothing but a trap, another form of warfare no different than AIDS."

Spring's viewpoint was intriguing, but to hear her break it down like that left him with only one question, "If you know it's a trap, why choose to work in that type of profession?"

Spring answered in one short sentence, "I have my reasons."

Though he wished she would have expounded more in-depth, he left it at that by drawing focus on his initial purpose for being there. "Not to deviate from our conversation, but you invited me to a home-cooked meal. What did you cook?"

"Nothing." She smiled, giving a sidelong, lascivious glance.

His face was tattooed with indecision. "I don't get it."

Spring leapt up and pushed him onto the bed. "I'm your dinner tonight."

Her statement sifted his inner-passion almost instantly. "An organic meal, how nice."

She had no rap, leaning forward to arrest his tongue with soft lips. Glued together by a sizzling rise in body heat, the kiss lasted for an eternity. Hands roamed freely, exploring each restricted area once deemed private property. Staring in each other's eyes, both were unquestionably caught in a moment of carnal pleasure. Bradshaw's heart pounded as she disrobed; Spring's chest haved as she tore his shirt open, becoming overly consumed by lust. While she caressed his manhood, he invaded her tight hole with two fingers. The shared energy was tantalizing.

Not being able to endure the teasing any longer, Bradshaw flipped Spring over and dived into her womanhood tongue first.

"Mmmmm, that feels so good," she whispered, seizing the back of his head with both hands.

Moans grew in volume as Bradshaw ate away, pushing her neatly- trimmed pussy into a throbbing climax.

"Yeeess! Yeeesss! Yeeeeeesssss!" shouted Spring, hypnotized by the wave of such a powerful orgasm.

Bradshaw continued licking her clitoris until the woman squealed like a wounded animal. With her legs still open, showing responsibility as a man, especially after hearing her take concerning children, he leaned over and fetched a condom. "Don't want to forget the jimmy hat," said Bradshaw in a selfless manner.

Spring waited impatiently, watching him slide on the rubber. As he slowly glided himself inside of her essence, she was absolutely pleased with his length and girth. It was the perfect fit. "Feels soooo good," Spring muttered.

Bradshaw begun to plow, giving his all to establish dominance. She bit his bottom lip, submitting to her lover's sexual thrashing. Five positions and several orgasms later, ninety minutes past in no time. Spring's final ery of bliss shoved Bradshaw over the edge, engineering the ultimate explosion on his behalf. Sweat-drenched, the satisfied couple collapsed, falling fast asleep without warning.

Bradshaw crept out of Spring's sheets while she was knee-deep in dreamland. Stripping himself from the gentle grip presented the ultimate challenge, but he had other business to dive into. Loyal to his routine, Bradshaw sped to the condo to grab the work and a hot shower. Catching every green light en route to Flag, he dropped the package off with ease, sent Spring a sweet text message, and landed at his job on time. As if walking on sunshine, he had a blast that entire morning, wearing happiness on his face until it was time to clock out. Joy gradually diminished the very second he spotted Jake leaning against the Fleetwood. His buddy's demeanor spelled everything but a peace of mind. Jake put a bug in Bradshaw's ear about the conversation he overheard in the barbershop. The info was alarming.

$ $ $ $

With a burning blunt pursed between his lips, Irvin was leafing through a mountain of cash when Bradshaw trampled in. He looked up, not really reading his mentor's vibe, and said, "Yo, dawg, we ain't accepting no more dollar bills. It takes up too much space. From now on the fiends gotta come with a solid ten or better. This shit don't make no sense."

Bradshaw joined Irvin on the carpet as the boy toiled to organize the pile into neat stacks. "Bro, our crew's name is buzzing. The 127 Building seemed to be breaking news inside the barbershop."

Irvin shooed it off as if the gossip was a good thing. "Wha'd you expect the people to say when we're banging their head like this." He flipped through a wicked stack of hundreds to justify the point. "Let the haters hate.

That's what they do best."

"I know that," Bradshaw's voice expressed urgency, "but Jake specifically told me that them niggas plotting."

That caught Irvin's attention. "Niggas as in who?"

"Tim-Tim, Willie D and some kids from up the hill named Kavy and Yancy."

Irvin gave him the skinny on the last two mentioned. "Kavy and Yancy are Grub's main head crackers. They whacked a lot of niggas for yo, and that's why he keeps their pockets fat."

In knowing Grub so well, Bradshaw considered himself an expert on the way his enemy thought, which meant he already deciphered Kavy and Yancy's position before gaining conformation. "I kind of already pieced that together. Well, they're targeting Sparky as the boss."

"Let'em," responded Irvin, dispassionately. "That keeps the focus off of us. That's what you said you wanted."

There were many mixed emotions, worst case scenarios took precedence that filled Bradshaw with regret. Theorizing a soundproof formula was much different than living it out. The reality of it all sucked.

"Yeah, but easier said than done. Since I agreed to sponsor this product, my name will eventually find their tongues."

Irvin carelessly shrugged, knowing in his heart that Bradshaw was damn well qualified to handle himself. Maybe it would take a situation like this to summon the savagery. "Heavy is the head that wears the crown. All we got to do is get this shipment off, one month, take it one day at a time. If it will keep you from sweating, I'll take some more artillery to the spot and put the crew on point."

That wasn't a solution to the problem, only a bandage. "Yeah, do that. I got a feeling shit is about to get crazy."

As he processed the new developments in his wig, Irvin promised, "And we'll be ready."

"You are still buying from Grub like I told you, right?"

Irving lied for the sake of dodging a tongue lashing. "Of course, I am."

Bradshaw commended his obedience. "Good work. They'll never know you're included. Now we'll just let the cards fall where they may."

Accepting an undeserved acclamation, while giving Grub the middle finger in his mind, Irvin doled a wry smile and continued to count.

$ $ $ $

Immediately after escorting a client to the waiting area, Spring quick stepped through a rear hallway to avoid crossing paths with

148

her perverted supervisor. There had been no communication between the two for quite some time, which multiplied Spring's guilt for reneging on her promise to him. She was usually a woman of her word, minus this case. Would she exchange sex for a favor, yes. For a trivial favor, no. In her yesteryears of club hopping from state to state, she strictly dealt with ballers, pawning off her cat to the highest bidder. But once faced with insurmountable odds, growing beyond her own shame, Spring thought of herself as one who learned from past mistakes. Though she wasn't wholly able to sail legit, finishing college advanced her maturity and self-worth, making her a master at what she secretly does best. Everyone had skeleton bones, but Spring used wisdom as a weapon against having her true craft exposed.

As Spring neared the center of the quiet hallway, a door to an empty sanitation closet spontaneously swung open. Before she could physically respond, Mr. Bart yanked her into the dark storage area, locking her arms with a tight grip.

"You've been using this deserted hall as a detour. Who'ya tryna dodge, huh?"

His mouth was so close to Spring's nose that she could smell the stench from his last cigarette break. "Get your weasel hands off of me."

"Or what..." He used his scrawny frame to pen her against the wall, squeezing her arms like a hungry reptile. "You tricked me out of that Peatican file for a reason. I know what you're up to. Now give me what I'm owed, or I'll blow your cover."

His statement stung Spring, jogging her mind to how carful she'd always been to not leave a trail of bread crumbs. And if Mr. Bart really had something on her, reliable ammunition he could have used to gain her panties, why wait until now to pull off an extortion stunt. Believing the chances of him just fishing for information, Spring called his bluff. "You don't know what you're talking about. Blow whatever you want, but I'll report your indecent behavior if you don't leave me alone."

Mr. Bart's face turned so red that it almost glowed in the dark. He became frantic. "Well I'll be sure to give you something to write in your complaint."

Rather than scream, Spring tried to strike him as she felt his hand go up her dress. He almost made it to her cookie before she kneed him in the nuts.

"Uuufff," he sighed, bowing in pain.

Spring opened the door and rushed out of the closet.

"I know where you live," Mr. Bart shouted as his prey expeditiously got away.

$ $ $ $

Collecting the loot, dropping off more guns and drugs, Irvin boogied after giving the crew a heads up. Following the brief meeting, soon as the sun hit the sky with a crossover, shit got funky in the projects. Ed was reprimanding a lazy look-out when a blue Caprice slowly spun the corner of the 127 Building. Ed peeped it in just enough time to whip out his pocket monster. As if the occupants behind the tinted windows spotted the nickel- plated pistol in his hand, the car came to an abrupt stop. Without any provocation, two men in mask jumped out with automatic rifles. In the midst of an environment saturated with fiends and residents, bangers went off like fireworks. Every shooter held their ground.

Taking cover behind a brick wall, Ed unloaded sixteen shots. Hearing and seeing the gunfight from the busted forth-floor window, even Fred engaged in the battle by blazing his rocket at the would-be assailants. The perilous fray lasted for no more than a minute. The crew's solidarity ultimately made the attackers retreat. With a Caprice now riddled with bullets, the car burned rubber. Out of all the trigger squeezing, miraculously, no one got hit. Scared bystanders survived yet another near death experience in a hood where innocent casualties usually resulted in these kind of violent feuds.

Ed sprung up the steps as he and Fred took shelter in Lisa's apartment. Chuckling nervously, Ed said, "Them wild coons almost peeled my cap."

Fred inhaled deeply. "Yeah, you was about to be a donut."

Ed didn't have to thank his comrade for popping off, going hard for each other came without saying. "Yo, we need to shut shop and let the heat die down."

"Yeah," Fred flipped open his cell, "and I'll call Sparky."

"Do that," said Ed, feeding the clip of his gun with more bullets as the sound of approaching sirens grew louder.

$ $ $ $

Irvin was about to stick dick to Vanessa when he got the chirp.

Sparky explained through the phone's walkie-talkie feature, "Some dudes got to buckin' shots at the crew, but everything cool. The Boys are heavy as uh whore out here."

Irvin rolled off of his girl. "Dog, just chill out until we get there."

"Say no more." Sparky disconnected.

Because of its sensitive nature, the incident couldn't be discussed over the phone. Showing up at their boss' doorstep meant serious business. As the two stood alone in front of Grub's suburban residence, Willie D whispered to his partner, "My nigga, them coons were on point. Soon as Kavy and Yancy hopped out the whip, bullets flew at us from all angles. Somebody tipped them off...I'm telling you."

Tim-Tim got fed up with Willie D while ringing the doorbell. "For the tenth time, you're right. You must get a kick out of me repeating myself."

"It got to be Jake because he was the only one around when we were connecting the dots. Don't you remember?"

"You're starting to sound like a fuckin' broken record," responded Tim-Tim, searching for the best method to relay the entire story to Grub.

Though vexed over the mission going sour, he still didn't feel the wrong call was made. Tim-Tim hoped Grub would understand.

"I keep mentioning yo name 'cause I can't wait to deal wit him."

Looking for someone, anyone to blame, Tim-Tim concurred, "He'll get his after we see what Grub says. For now just shut up and follow my lead."

When a foyer light came on from inside the villa, the men caught butterflies and almost fell weak at the knees. Both had a lot of explaining to do.

$ $ $ $

When Bradshaw and Irvin got to the 127 Building, there were no squad cars, yellow crime-scene tape nor white chalk circling spun-shell casings. Had the projects been a privileged community, a shoot-out of that magnitude would have made the news. But in this case, the hood was at ease and back to normal. However, contrary to the outside environment, Sparky had the crew in an uproar as he voiced his opinion.

"I say we give that fat chump a taste of his own medicine, fight fire with fire. He got the steps in the 107 and 126 Buildings. We should shoot his shit up to let him see we ain't nothing to be fucked with."

Bradshaw was cool as a fan when he replied, "When it comes to selling drugs, shoot-outs and money don't mix. No need to be on a warpath, keep y'all minds on business. I'll personally deal with the rest."

Sparky blurted, "You ain't the one who got shot at."

Irvin spoke up for his Top dawg, "And neither were you."

Still furious, Sparky put his head down, eyes shooting upward. "We're thriving in a dangerous neighborhood amongst beast who only respects strength. If we let this slide, they'!l think we're pussy and try us again. Flag feeds off violence, and that's why an example has to be set, stating we bust heads, too."

Though giving Sparky a reprimanding look, Bradshaw did feel his point of view. "Dawg, just stick to the script and stay focus. Earn your keep. I'm not paying yall to think or be a strategist. That's my department. Y'all know about my work in the past. I'm not soft, only wiser. There's a lot ridig on us making this money. Trust my judgment and don't worry about what the hood thinks. Little do y'all know, we're wiping out the competition wit the quantity and quality of our crack alone. When war time arrives, Ill be the one to let y'all know. Each of you need to hear and obey."

The crew listened and stayed quiet the whole time. Complying with nods of approval illustrated their obedience to Bradshaw's leadership.

As much as it slaughtered Sparky to come to terms with a nonviolent approach, majority ruled. He tucked his tail and went with the flow, saying to Bradshaw and Irvin, "I'm loyal to the cause, follow y'all all the way. But when the opportunity presents itself, I won't hesitate to set the example."

Bradshaw appreciated his courage but wasn't impressed. Anyone could pop a gun; furthermore, a killer knew how to shoot, but a true murderer knew when to shoot. That's what separated him from his angst lieutenant.

The crew dispersed after being instructed to take the night off, but Sparky was held back to escort his two big-hats downstairs.

When the three got on the elevator, Bradshaw checked Sparky, "Make that your last time questioning me, let alone in front of them. You are part of this family's leadership branch; therefore, you must remember to separate yourself from the soldiers. Never let them see you out of control."

Sparky ate the lashing, adamantly responding, "You're right, won't happen again."

Irvin gave him something to think about. "I brought you to the table because your potential to lead. But every good leader was once a great follower. We're not trying to hold you down; we want to see you floss and get money. Who knows, if you play your position, someday you might be the one pulling all the strings."

Sparky knew it was in his cards to become a boss, and he would fulfill his calling with or without them. "I feel you on that. Since I know where I went wrong, consider it already fixed."

And just that easy, the topic became water under the bridge. When they walked out of the building, Bradshaw noticed Kenya sliding out of a Q45. Judging by her short skirt and flimsy top, she had the trashy appearance of a female who just finished freaking off. With that instantaneously getting under his skin, Bradshaw forgot about Irvin and Sparky as he made a beeline over to his sister. "You're gonna stop disrespecting yourself in my sight."

She barked back, "Get the hell out of my face. I do what I want. You are not my father or man."

The driver-side door of the Q45 swung open. A red dude in a jogging suit stepped from the car. He lifted his shirt to expose the butt of a handgun. "Don't get your shit split by running up on my car like that."

Even though he himself wasn't strapped, Bradshaw didn't cower. "Yo, mind your business. This is my sister."

"And that's my side bitch, which is the only reason I ain't burn you the fuck up yet," explained the boy.

Kenya got between them, begging her friend to get back in the car. "Yella, just leave, you don't have to explain nothing to him."

Sparky and Irvin surveyed the little squabble from not even a yard away. Neither spotted the butt of Yella's gun from the angle where they stood. But when the boy whipped it out, Sparky jumped into action.

"You see this in my hand," Yella cocked the hammer to make a point, "I could end you right here, dawg."

"I'm not scared of no gun." Bradshaw remained firm as his sister continuously pled for Yella to roll out. "Go ahead and use it."

Kenya's friend never seen Sparky creeping up on him. Finally having the chance to stand on his own words, Sparky made an example with four shots blasting at the side of Yella's head.

[BOOOOM! BOOOOM! BOOOOM! BOOOOM!]

Every bullet landed in Yella's skull. The impact knocked the boy's lifeless body sideways, causing it to collapse between the door of the Q45. When Kenya screamed, Sparky grabbed the shining pistol out of Yella's hand and split into the building. The situation went down so fast that it was over before the crew even knew what happened. Bradshaw ushered his hysterical sister to the Lexus as nosy bystanders congregated, playing detective as they always did. A gunfight earlier, then this; the police were sure to camp out for the duration of the night.

Immediately upon the Lexus exiting the slums, Sparky received a buzz from Irvin instructing him to lay low for awhile. There was no telling who saw what. And for the best interest of the crew, Irvin committed himself to supervising the steps until further notice. Sparky wasn't feeling that one bit.

$ $ $ $

Spring dazed off while applying an avocado masque in her vanity mirror. Tense from being literally rubbed the wrong way at work, her brain raced back to how her journey started. Being raised in Lafayette Projects introduced her to all the tricks of the trade, the highs and lows of poverty. By the time her parents moved her out of the hood at seventeen, it was already too late to begin again.

The sin committed behind project walls haunted them. When Mom and Dad were arrested on conspiracy charges, both sentenced to life in federal prison, she was left to fend for herself and six-year-old brother. Tough times forced them back into the hood. Refusing to bitch and gripe, Spring did what she had to do to put food on the table. While maintaining a 3.5 grade average in school, she worked at several strip clubs on Baltimore Street. Exotic dancing even landed her in Miami for a short spell. As time went on, she grew attracted to fast cash. Choosing to sell pussy rather than narcotics became her cup of tea, and juicing men was like a second nature.

Spring accumulated enough scratch to foot her own tuition, Learning the art of computer hacking from a friend in college, she tested the waters of her new craft by stealing identities, receiving credit cards in the same names and maxing out. When that reached boredom, Spring stepped it up and created a foolproof identity theft racket. Running the entire operation from her desktop, with the cyber world fairly new back then, she pocketed over two million dollars within the first eighteen months of launching her illegal enterprise.

Spring's hustle was so effective because she only stole the identities of individuals locked up. She even choose to be a parole agent because it placed her in the perfect position to screen potential victims. Though her business ran smooth since day one, she felt it was time to move on due to all the new technology being created to combat identity theft. Recently graduating to money laundering, placing currency in real-estate, uncut diamonds and oil stocks, Spring currently had four million invested in assets and another seven million wrapped up in offshore accounts. Spring was at such a boss level in her career, not forgetting where she came from, an important service of washing dirty money was ready to be extended to the underworld. Charging just 10%, she was certain the profits would be very lucrative.

As wonderful as all this sounded, she had one problem: no protection on the streets. This was where Bradshaw fitted into the equation. From the second she saw his name on the entry docket at the office, capitalizing off of his muscle became a must. Made men knew who he was and how he got down. Feared by enemies and loved by friends, Spring believed Bradshaw would be the perfect front. What she didn't factor in was falling in love with him so hard, so fast; nevertheless, business came first. If Bradshaw was the discreet king she imagined him to be, he'd be offered the keys to her castle, for having him on her team was a half-won battle. But if he proved to be reckless, she'd just enjoy his company until he got knocked back off by the police.

As far as her supervisor was concerned, before she allowed her plans to be compromised, or even feel unsafe inside her own pad,

Bart would find himself in a funeral home. Making that sacrifice was worth watching her plan march forward.

Spring shook out of her momentary stupor and ran some hot bath water.

CHAPTER 9

In all the hardship Bradshaw was confronted with since being ejected from prison, nothing matched watching a guy get his brains blown out over stupidity. It made him reflect on the shallow excuses he himself used to kill in the past, wondering how many more would die as a consequence of crossing his path. Oppose to feeling any semblance of remorse, he experienced shedding fear associated with the tragic outcome of living that street life. But if he could perfect his endgame, play it smart by outthinking the enemy, there was hope in making it to the other side of the rainbow, unscathed.

Through the complicated process of nursing Kenya out of shock, Bradshaw extracted intricate details pertaining to the murdered victim. If all his sister said was true, based solely on Yella's popularity and clout in Park Heights, his boys were going to want revenge. As it stood, ducking war was virtually impossible unless the shooter remained a mystery. Avoiding smoke with one of the most strongest hoods in Baltimore was essential to accomplishing his goal. While plotting the best solution to deflect future bloodshed, Bradshaw stared off into the darkness of his room until day broke.

Since Bradshaw couldn't be at two places at once, he called out sick from work. As a rule of thumb, he had to keep both ears to the concrete in order to accurately access his next move as commander and chief. What better place to gather information then at the barbershop. If its rumor-mill was churning, hell of niggas would be inside scuttle-butting like women. Kenya was ordered to stay at the condo until he was sure she'd be safe moving around.

Bradshaw parked directly behind Flag House Projects, in Little Italy, which was an Italian neighborhood known for its mob ties. He strutted to his destination just to find out the barbershop was closed. That was a first. It not being open for business spoke volumes. Since he couldn't get his ears greased that way, Bradshaw had to rely on Kia's graduation on upcoming Saturday.

Grub would be front and center. That golden opportunity would be used to expend his promised favor and personally let Grub know the crew, in the 127 Building, belonged to him. With Grub being made conscious, Bradshaw wanted him to back off while they dealt with Yella's beef, for the crew couldn't handle a battle with both forces at the same time.

As Bradshaw walked back to Little Italy, a brown Crown Victoria crept up alongside him. He knew a police car when he seen one. *Multiple antenna's were a dead giveaway.* With the driver side of the vehicle facing the curb, the dark window eased down revealing an officer behind the wheel. It was the same Housing Cop who sent him to prison. Bradshaw's tone was venomous when he asked, "What the fuck do you want, Butcher? I'm not in the game no more. I work."

Butcher slammed the car in park an jumped out, imposingly. At 250lbs. of solid muscle, and at 6'6", the detective looked like he ate weights for breakfast, lunch and dinner. "Naw, ain't heard dat one; matter-of-fact, I was told the opposite. They say you back in business."

Bradshaw huffed and puffed as he was forced against the police car.

"You heard wrong. Maybe you should feed your rats better cheese to score better info."

While frisking his subject, Butcher uttered, "When I heard you was out, my cock got hard. I ain't put a major case together in a long time. I'm sure you're tied to some illegal activity in the projects; I can feel it in my bones."

As the desperate cop ransacked his pockets, Bradshaw muttered, "You got me messed up. I'm clean."

"So you say." He turned Bradshaw around to face him. "A lot of shit has changed through the years. Thanks to your conviction, they shot me straight to the top. Becoming the head detective of a Housing Authority. "'m no longer a Jump-Out Boy. Not only do I run my own task force but I also been promoted with Federal Deputization. There's a slew of veteran prosecutors eating out of my hands, which mean I'm in a grand position to make your life a living hell."

Bradshaw hated Butcher ten times more than Grub. "Find something more fruitful to do with your credentials besides harassing innocent people over their past lifestyles. Niggas can change."

After not finding any drugs or guns on Bradshaw's person, he shoved him to the side with an aggressive shoulder bump and got back into the Crown Victoria. "I got my eyes on you."

Bradshaw grabbed at his own crotch, shaking it as the cop got low. He came to the conclusion this encounter was a real problem, one that threaten his freedom in the worse way.

$ $ $ $

The morning was chill, and the sky peaceful over Port Street. Nothing was unusual to neighbors who came and went on their regular schedules. But behind the doors of the only brown house on the block, death angels assembled to prepare for a potential snatch and grab. Strapped in a chair with both hands fastened behind his back, eyes nearly bruised shut, Jake appealed to his attackers, "I'm suffering for nothing. I don't know what you talking "bout, swear!"

Not buying it, Willie D yelled in his face, "You ratted to them coons after ear-fucking our conversation. We're no dummies."

Refusing to cross Bradshaw for Grub, Jake endured a few more solid blows to the mug. "Y'all making a mistake. I had nothing to do with it. I paid no attention to your so-called conversation at the shop."

Tim-Tim settled at the theorem Jake would probably take the truth to his grave. For the sake of catering to another interest of his boss's curiosity, he presented an important question, "We might let you walk out in one piece, that's only if you tell us were those 127 Building Boys working for Yella?"

Jake truly didn't have that scoop. "I can't tell you something I don't know."

Willie D dove back into his ass with well-coordinated blows.

As the thrashing continued, Grub stood behind the action, chin high, looking the part of a successful street pharmacist. They'd been in the house for an hour with no results. Patience fading, he had enough of observing Tim-Tim and Willie D expend energy beating a dead horse. Pausing the attack,

Grub stepped forward and stared down at the weeping man, "I always liked you. Be smart. Don't lose your life over nothing. Dawg, I forgive you for blabbering to them dudes. Shit happens. Just tell me what Yella was doing down the 'Jects if he wasn't picking up money."

Nose gushing blood, Jake looked up at him with a hunch of the shoulders, ignorance filled his eyes.

Reading his facial expression as that of a fool who refused to give in, Grub gave Jake his back. "Them kids been pumping work in Flag without my permission. Yella was their plug. Like the crutty little bastards they are, those kids probably got greedy and smashed him, that alone is gonna shut them down. Shorty had that long dope money. Maybe we don't have to flush them out after all. Park Heights will handle our dirty work."

"The enemy of our enemy is our friend," said Willie D, laughing aloud.

Grub smirked. "I guess I'll be needing a new barber."

It was that short sentence which caught Jake's ear. He knew exactly what that meant. "I'm cooperating the best I can. We all cool. Don't do this to me, man. Please..."

After listening to Jake beg for his life, every word that followed became a blur. With a nod of the head, Grub gave Tim-Tim the okay to finish him off.

"Grub! Grub!" shouted Jake as the fat man left the room.

Tim-Tim exposed a large bottle of gorilla glue. "I'm sure this will keep your mouth permanently shut."

Willie D put Jake in a headlock as the thick glue was squeezed down his throat.

$ $ $ $

Bradshaw missed Spring so bad that he dropped in on her without an appointment. Soon as she spotted his name on the sign-in sheet, he was immediately called to the back. She appeared just as happy to see him as he was to see her. The two would have embraced had they not been at her job.

Spring cheesed as if she was on a photo shoot. "Don't you hate this place enough on Mondays? What brings you to Parole and Probation on Friday? I wasn't expecting this surprise visit."

"I needed to see your pretty face," uttered Bradshaw, slowly inhaling her hypnotizing scent.

She melted in her seat. "That's so sweet."

He should have chased her response down with a smile; instead, the man looked away wearing the stress of life on his face.

Spring detected his inner perplexity without labor, decoding all that his lips wasn't saying. Concerned to the max, she asked, ""What's the matter, boo? Why the twitchy eyes?"

Impressed by her keen ability to read him, he tried to play it off. "I'm alright, it's nothing."

She didn't let him off the hook. "I graduated with a minor in psychiatry. It's my business to study people, so don't tell me nothing is wrong."

Wishing he could use Spring's arms for a therapeutic recliner, relax and purge his mind of every troubled thought, Bradshaw attempted to manage a fatigued smile. "I don't want to bore you with my problems. I can handle it on my own."

Spring scoffed. "Don't sidestep to maintain a tough image. Let down your shield and talk to me."

Her persistence had him sold. "It's not like I don't want to talk, but right now ain't the time. It's too much to break down...wouldn't know where to start."

She realized her office wasn't a place that made him comfortable enough to delve into specifics. The right setting could possibly help him open up. "Want to come chill with me tonight? We can use that time to have a heart-to-heart and get to know each other better. I believe we both have personal issues that haven't been discussed."

He felt Spring had the perfect life, an open-and-shut book, featuring a real angel on earth. Her personal issues couldn't be heavier than his.

In need of her comfort, he conceded. "That sounds wonderful."

Spring wanted to feel his lips so bad. "I told you I was here if or whenever you need me."

"It means a lot to hear you reiterate that."

"It feels even better to have you accepting mental and emotional support."

His eyes finally found hers. ""What's nice comes twice, I guess."

Not wanting his impromptu visit to raise suspicion, she kept it short and sweet. "You better go, but I will be waiting on you tonight."

Bradshaw stood to leave. "No doubt."

Mr. Bart watched from a distance as Spring escorted her client out. His anger bubbled to the point of no return. He whispered to himself, *'Fool me once, shame on you. It won't be a second time.'*

$ $ $ $

In front of Mason Ct., down Perkins Projects, stomping and raving, Sparky hissed a fit in his little cousin's ear, "I didn't blam dude for a pat on the back; I squeezed off on principle. And according to my job title, that's not even my duty. As a reward for stepping up to the plate, them scary-ass niggas put me on ice. I can't believe that shit."

As he helped his big cuzo chug a brew, Lunchbox shook his head fervently. Just in a ten minute conversation, Sparky already revealed major facts as to who he was hustling for. Lunchbox put two and two together that Bradshaw had to be the dude who showed face with Irvin at the playground. Sympathizing with his cousin's dilemma had no bearing on his own rage concerning not being chose as a candidate to spearhead the new shop. *Why didn't Irvin put him down with the crew?* That was some bonified bullshit from Lunchbox's viewpoint. He spoke mostly out of spite, "That nigga Irvin is a phony busta. You got to expect him to trade on you. He was even hitting me with some rocks on the low and cut me off for no reason."

Sparky looked Lunchbox up and down. "Oh, yeah...y'all called yourselves hiding that from me?"

Knowing how Sparky felt about him grinding in the streets, especially after keeping him under the wing since a cub, Lunchbox lied in his attempt to add coal to the fire, "It was Irvin's idea."

He popped the boy upside the cranium. "I told my aunt, on her deathbed, I'd look out for you, but I can't keep that promise if you out here being sneaky, keeping stupid secrets."

"But —"

"Shut up," demanded Sparky. "What the hell I told you about pitching stones?"

[Lunchbox went to shrug but was caught with another pop upside the head.]

Sparky answered his own question, "I said niggas don't play fair. They'll pimp you to get ahead, have you take all the big chances for small pennies. If you are ever to hustle, it'll be with me. I'll make sure you get some real money. That simple."

His only good eye dove south. "You know my lead bands is about to drop, and we can put the whole check on copping a few bricks. After we take over the city, we can push Irvin and Bradshaw out of the mix."

In agreement, Sparky used the carrot-on-a-rope as a bargaining tool to give Lunchbox something to look forward to. "I'm wit it, but we'll fuck that cat when it comes,"

Lunchbox rubbed his palms together so fast both hands would have caught on fire had they been made of wood. "I can't wait."

Sparky put the brew up to his lips, saying before swallowing down the last drop, "That nigga Irvin think he slick giving you work without pulling my coat about it first. I got his bad ass. He'll get his karma in due time. I ain't trippin'."

This was the first Friday Bradshaw postponed his usual outing with Doobie. He traveled to Spring's house in place of his son's. He arrived at her home to find the rich aroma of baked Tilapia in the air. Following that tasty meal and some hardcore sex, the couple cuddled as the moon spied with just enough light to fasten them into a post-romantic mood.

"You feel so good, so right," whispered Bradshaw, holding her tight.

"Ditto," she purred, Even in the ecstasy of the moment, Spring sensed his uneasiness and that tugged at her heart. She had a feeling that whatever was bothering him might've been associated with the game. Though he never mentioned dibbling and dabbling back into his old habits, Spring knew the symptoms, for she experienced the same enigmatic energy with her parents before they went bye-bye. Deep inside, she couldn't knock the hustle. The suspense was a bummer. "Are you ready to share what's running through that mind of yours?"

Even in a secured bedroom, with just them two present, Bradshaw squirmed as if being watched by an audience.

She made light of his jitters. "It's okay, baby. You can keep it real with me. I won't violate your parole."

Smothering an oncoming guffaw, Bradshaw doled a chip-toothed smile. "Ha-ha-ha, very funny. Right."

She got back on serious time. "We're better than this. Our relationship will never grow if we don't learn to trust each other. Communication is the first step to establishing trust, so cough it up."

Her perspective on trust was good shit, but he didn't want to present an image that would make her look at him differently. If he brought up the shootout, Yella getting trashed, the potential beef with Park Heights, drugs and Butcher, all of that would be too heavy to lay on Spring in one swing. In fact, everything wasn't for everybody. But not wanting her to feel like he wasn't willing to give trust a chance, Bradshaw selected to expose the shallow end of his problems. "I'm stressed because not only is my twin sisters off the hook but my other sister, Kia, who's about to graduate from Law School on Saturday, deals with Grub and is set to marry him in the near future. That alone gets me heated. Besides that, my mother and father get high. I'm starting to hate my job, and I'm having nightmares about prison."

Though Spring felt he was ducking and dodging the real truth of his confused emotions, she patiently listened, then said, "Your thoughts are everywhere. It all sounds like one huge run-on sentence, no commas, no periods. The best method to solving a problem is learning how to separate your thoughts. Organize them by categories, and attack one at a time. This makes finding a solution that much easier."

Bradshaw sighed as her hand found its way around his chest. Spring's words were well spoken, each syllable landing with precision. Tethered to the street code, no matter how accurate the advice, he still abstained from sharing incriminating information, At this point, questions were better than statements. "So, what would you do if you was me?"

She spoke slow in order to camouflage the swiftness of her mind, "I can't give you an accurate solution to your problems. Only you can do that. I'm just here to help you look within self and make the right choices. Don't let your family be the reason you fall off or lose focus. They were out here thriving when you were away, and their lives won't stop if you go back to prison. Keep your eyes on the prize."

He loved the way she broke that down. Too bad her advice didn't speak to the real obstacles that threatened his existence. "I'll use your formula to deal with my issues. See, that quick," he snickered, "I feel better already."

Spring heard Bradshaw's lips talking but detected no shift in his energy. A person didn't have to love a lie to live it. If he wasn't willing to wholeheartedly open up to her, she for damn sure wasn't going to be the first to expose her hand. Yearning for a more worthy incentive to go the distance, praying for him to let his wall down so she could pop the big question, Spring gave him another chance to clean it up. "Are you sure there's nothing else troubling you?"

As casual as he responded, Bradshaw might as well been sitting cross- legged, puffing a cigar when he said, "Nah, that's it."

Even with much doubt in his tone, that wasn't what she hoped to hear. Spring couldn't take a leap of faith with a man who wasn't ready to keep it one hundred. Until he opened up completely, her underworld operation remained at a standstill. Adjourning all she prepared to lay on him about her business proposition, Spring ended their discourse with a bit of universal law. "This is your life. Don't half step. If you're going to strive for success, stomp with both feet. Put your all into it. You can't afford to fail!"

Being shot with those words, it was in that moment Bradshaw chose to stop bluffing in the street. If the game was craving for the old him, it would get just that. Fight fire with fire...that was the solution. He thanked her with a kiss, allowing her to turn with her back facing him.

Stuck in her own head, Spring stared at the wall in silence as they spooned.

$ $ $ $

Tyson picked up the torch after the untimely slaying of his predecessor. He would have sent a handful of desperados down Flag House to twist arms, popping some heads, but that was less satisfying then blasting his own gun. Even with the same killer instinct as Yella, Tyson wasn't as flashy or loud. He was a kid who took pride in connecting all the dots before making a move.

Allowing an enemy to think the beef was dead, then strike from he blindside, was his trump. The extra tip gained from a mole, some new names mentioned had yet been proven, but he took the names into consideration. So far, he knew Flag House was Grub's territory, and chances were Grub had the wire on how and why Yella got hit. Kenya's name was never brought up due to Yella finding her too insignificant to openly acknowledge.

Tyson looked at Rabbit as the teenager loaded the AK-47. "That assault rifle is just as tall as you. When the time come for you to buck that bitch, I hope it don't break your shoulder or some shit."

Rabbit was fourteen with a baby face that said ten. He was Yella's only biological sibling, rumored to have killed more dudes than Tyson and Yella combined. Shorty was the one. "You know me, I rather creep down on ah nigga with something small, all head shots. But now I'm on some Rambo shit. Them niggas killed my brother, gloves off. I'm dirtin' them and whoever else they love."

Rabbit was indeed a little nigga with a big heart. Tyson could not have had a better person by his side. "I'm on the same time. Once we find out who did it, we gonna hit'um where it hurt. That's my word."

CHAPTER 10

Irvin supervised the steps a full week without incident. No shootouts, no drama, just a steady flow of cash. The good thing was that the connect's bill was almost reached. The only rough obstacle was how time consuming it was to stay posted in one spot from sun to moon. It seemed as though time apart was injuring Irvin and Vanessa's relationship. Infact, her opinion was that he was out cheating with another woman. Since she was the only way to the plug, he couldn't leave her stuck inside the condo, unhappy. Kenya kept her company for a few days until she was back out-and-about. After getting sick of listening to Vanessa crying to him about not being sheltered with comfort, Irvin put Sparky back on the job. His lieutenant was compensated with a raise and double pay for pain and suffering.

Outside of step business, Jake's death was the latest breaking news in the hood. When Bradshaw heard about it, he cried like an infant. Though it couldn't be proven, his gut said it was Grub's work. Jake did a noble deed by warning them about the plot, but that wasn't worth him closing his eyes for good. Straight guilt ate at Bradshaw's core. A huge part of him was determined to ride for Jake. Someway, somehow. He would not let Jake's death be in vain. That was the fleeting thought on his mind as he dressed Saturday morning for Kia's graduation.

Subsequent to ringing Peaches, a few rap songs later Bradshaw's whip was perched in front of her home. A four minute horn-assault finally extracted Doobie from within the house. A color scheme of cream and brown had his son clean for the event, but when Doobie hopped into the car, it was obvious that Peaches hacked his head with the clippers. Even though the cut was botched, it was presentable, nonetheless. Making a mental note to do better, Bradshaw blamed self for every noticeable flaw in Doobie's appearance.

He opened the back door for his son and asked, "How you been doing?"

Doobie answered as he buckled himself in, "Good."

To keep from generating mixed signals, Bradshaw resisted the temptation to inquire about Peaches' current status. If she had a new boyfriend or not, it wasn't any of his business since he chose other than her. Instead of building on Peaches, Bradshaw used that opportunity to introduce Spring's name. Doobie asked personal questions about the mystery woman en route to Bowie, but when she got in the car, her glow spoke for itself.

Spring kissed Bradshaw and looked toward the back seat. "Hello, handsome."

Her beauty gave him a sugar rush. "Wow, you're pretty."

Caught by the swift blow of his blunt appraisal, she was flattered. "Thank you. Nice to see that you and dad share the same taste."

Still spellbound, he replied, "I'm Doobie."

Her eyes glittered like falling stars. "Oh, I already know all about you. Meeting you in the flesh is a real pleasure."

Doobie took a leap. "You love my father?"

She pinched him on the cheek. "I sure do."

"Ooooh." A taste of disappointment was present.

Spring read him quickly, soothing his mind like a true veteran. "It's quite natural to want your parents together, but that don't have to stop you and I from becoming friends, does it?"

The disheartened child thought about it for a second, heavy eyes shooting over at his father and then back at her. "No...I guess we can be friends."

Treating him like a miniature boss, she shook Doobie's hand. "Well, friends we are."

Impressed by how easily Spring won his son over, Bradshaw kept all comments to himself. When he got to the Georgetown Auditorium, the place was packed. It took fifteen minutes to find a parking spot. Bradshaw felt like a fish in a sea of white folks, that was until he seen his family seated in the front row. His mom, dad and the twins were sitting right next to Grub, Tim-Tim and Willie D. Since it was Kia's day, tension and animosity were pushed under the table. Fake smiles, daps and hugs were shared and received.

While Cathy and the twins doted over Doobie, Grub leaned back and whispered to Bradshaw, "Yo, when this ceremony over, I got some rap for you."

Instead of conversing, Bradshaw wanted to knock Grub's head off, but he maintained composure, responding cordially, "Same here. I got some rap for you as well."

Nods were exchanged and that was that.

Ocky could've sent a lookout to grab a bite for the steps, but they never got the orders right. *How hard was it to remember no cheese or mayo on his shit?* So, instead of leaving the fate of his starving belly in the hands of an air-head geeker, he took a short break from the steps to personally snatch lunch for the day-shift crew. Since Ocky planned it to be an in-and-out activity, he chose not to tote a strap. It was just his luck to get pinched by

Housing Authority while making a fast run. "Not da'day," he whispered to himself, dashing to a neighborhood carryout.

Jumping in front of a short line of hungry negroes, he ordered cold cuts and chips to keep his visit snappy. Waving off the angry chatters of those who didn't appreciate his inconsiderate actions, Ocky bopped to the rear of the store and popped two quarters inside an arcade. With his back towards the only entrance, he engaged in a game of Centipede to stay occupied until his number was called. Ocky's brain got so enthralled in the game, he never seen the two dudes creeping up behind him.

By the time Ocky looked up, he was already caught slipping.

It was late noon when Kia walked across the stage. Though family hooped and hollered, she smiled, hugging the dean without a speech. And just like that, since she was the last to accept her degree, the formal portion of the ceremony was over. Bradshaw and Grub broke away from everyone else, taking to a quiet corner in the reception area. The fat man lit a cigar and initiated the conversation by once again apologizing for the past.

"Brah, my bad for fucking up our bond. Truth be told, when you got bumped, I was lost out here, then started making bigger moves and got bull- headed, forgot where I came from. By time I came to my senses, you was already disgusted with me. I didn't want to make matters worse, so I kept it pushing."

Bradshaw didn't buy a word he said. Grub had the hood faked out but not him. All that Al Capone shit was a facade. It was his reputation Grub used to gain universal respect. It was no secret Grub owed him, and, just as he planned, Bradshaw played on it to his advantage. "Yeah, you fucked me over, but you did right by my sister. That counts for something in my book. On the strength of that, the hatchet is buried between you and I."

That was music to Grub's ears. "No doubt. That's big love coming from you."

Bradshaw continued to gild the lily, "Everybody must grow sometime.

As family, we can't get stuck on the bad. Let's focus on the good and move on. Build...know what I'm saying?"

Illiterately reading between the lines, Grub selfishly thought Bradshaw was ready to get back down and dirty with him. "I got as much work as you need. Just say the word."

"Nah," Bradshaw took a step back with a shake of the head, "I need something legit. I was thinking you should let me buy that barbershop around the way."

Grub squinted, using an extended pause as an indication of befuddlement.

Bradshaw redoubled his efforts. "Remember what you said about that promise in the car?"

Standing on his word, Grub spoke as if a gap in thought hadn't existed. "I do. If the barbershop is your goal, you can have that."

"For free?" Bradshaw gave stern eye contact.

"Of course. No problem. I'll sign it over to you bright Monday morning."

Bradshaw knew bullshit was coming. "What's the catch?"

Grub proceeded without a blink, "Them boys in the 127 Building bit off more than they can chew. I know they had something to do with Yella getting blasted. Park Heights niggas gearing up for war, and I don't want them to aim guns at the wrong folks. Irvin cool with them niggas in the 127 Building, and you tight with him."

"Your point is?"

"All 'm saying is don't get jammed up in that shit."

Bradshaw fished, "But ain't Irvin still copping from you?"

"Hell no! I haven't heard anything from him in nearly a month."

So Irvin lied, *Bradshaw thought to himself.* "'m green to that whole getty-up. Tell me what makes you sure them kids had something to do with Yella?"

"Because them kids moving big shit. How could they have enough work to run a 24-hour shop? If they ain't getting it from me, Yella was the only other heavy hitter who could supply that kind of demand."

At last Bradshaw seen the complete picture for what it was. The Park Heights nigga's mind wasn't on the 127 Building. It was on Grub, and he needed a scapegoat. Yella was Grub's chief competitor, and him getting killed down Flag House meant one thing: Grub ordered the hit. Rightfully so, if the blame could be shifted to Sparky and the crew, two birds would ultimately kill themselves with one stone. Bradshaw smelt game and decided not to reveal his hand until after Monday. "Them kids down the hood respect me. Maybe I can get close to them to see what's up. Loose lips sink ships. They'll slip up and brag if they did it."

Appearing a bit relieved, Grub replied, "That's the business, but how long do you think it'll take to pick their brains?"

Attempting to buy more time to move the rest of the package without strain, Bradshaw retorted, "A few weeks, maybe..."

"Why so long?"

"I can't just roll up out the blue asking who killed Yella. That's some hot shit."

Grub gave it a thought. "True."

"I'll take care of it as I always have. Us family got to look out for each other."

Tapping his cigar out at the halfway mark, his only real concern was self. "Do what you do, and report back to me with some specifics. I'll bless you beyond signing the shop over if need be. I got you, and you got me."

The fact Jake's name was never mentioned said it all. Bradshaw was convinced beyond a reasonable doubt Grub killed poor Jake, and that tore him apart on the inside. "We'll fox these niggas out together. Just like old times."

Grub couldn't help but give Bradshaw a hug. "I love when we're on the same side. Hey, meet me downtown by ten on Monday. Here's the address."

Taking the info, Bradshaw decided against pulling away. The stage was set.

$ $ $ $

A long day of making lasting impressions on Bradshaw's family concluded with Spring and Doobie swapping hugs and goodbyes. Bradshaw intently watched from the car as his son ran inside the house. Floating on the slow beat of old-school jams on the radio, the energy was perfect between the couple, that was until Bradshaw turned the music down to take a call from his little homie.

Irvin shouted into the phone, "Yo, Brad, Ocky missing. He left the steps to grab some food and never came back. A fiend said they saw something but didn't say what, yet. We squeezing him right this second. We need you down the projects now!"

Irvin was so loud Bradshaw was sure Spring heard every word. There was no way to conceal the fact that something was terribly wrong. "Bro, say less, be to you shortly."

In a blast of anger, Irvin ranted on, "I swear, these niggas about to catch the blues if Ocky don't turn up. I mean it!"

"You said enough. Chill until I get there. I'm on my way," said Bradshaw, hanging up to spare the ears of his passenger. He was so busted.

Spring looked more worried than shocked. "What is that all about?"

He played it down in one last attempt to conceal his dark side.

"Nothing much. See...Ocky is my homeboy's pooch. The damn dog must of climbed out of the yard again and got lost. Irvin need me to help find him..."

Spring wasn't stupid. She knew that urgent call was wrapped around some raw-street shit and became offended over him insulting her intelligence.

"You would sit in my face and lie, treat me like a green bean who don't know both sides of the coin. That's totally messed up."

Parking in her driveway, Bradshaw peered out the windshield with a dumbfounded expression, favoring a deer caught in headlights.

Spring intrusively dug, "Don't be like other men with no heart for true love. They end up losing more than that little, phony pooch you referred to."

"Baby." He reached for her.

She recoiled. "All I ask for is the unadulterated truth. You don't have to be afraid to trust me. I'm sick of all this marry-go-round kid shit. Be straight up. I can handle it."

That was his first time hearing Spring use profanity, which proved she was certainly beside herself. In respect to her feelings, he said, "Okay, you got me. There are thing's going on in my life you don't know about, and to protect you...I thought it best to keep it that way."

"Some protection," she muttered, sarcastically.

"Baby, I —"

"So now you want to admit you haven't been honest?"

He was in a frenzy, gasping for the right words to cool her off. "You looking at it the wrong way."

His opinion amounted to straight gibberish at that point. "I already knew you were out here doing God knows what, and that call proved it. We all got secrets, but why be in a relationship if two people can't relate?"

He continued to justify his actions, "Sometimes secrets are necessary. There's no fun in playing Spades with the cards up."

"But that's where your wrong; what we share isn't a game." Spring opened the car door, sucking her teeth. "And until you're ready to spread those so-called cards across the table, I suggest we be friends, nothing exclusive."

"I think you are over-reacting —"

"You heard what I said. Don't let this tough stuff be the reason you lose your blessing." Believing a cold shoulder would surely cut through his thick shell, hopefully more sooner than later, Spring concluded their conversation by bolting from the car in what resembled a fit of rage.

Instead of giving chase, he pulled from the driveway. With important business to handle down the projects, Bradshaw didn't have another minute to spare. He and Spring's relationship would have to be mended at a later date.

$ $ $ $

The tension was high at the 127 Building by the time Bradshaw touched down. Every member of the crew was on edge. While Sparky and Tabo ran the step operation, Ed posted up outside the forth-floor stairwell holding a Street-Sweeper. On the first floor of the steps was Fred with an AK-47 locked and loaded. Bradshaw found Irvin inside Lisa's house also with a gun in hand, interrogating a neighborhood fiend who went by the name of

Blackface. He was an old-school dude who kept up with the new fashion but favored a housefly. Blackface usually served as one of Grub's lookouts in the 107 Building. It was unclear why Blackface was on his knees, crying real tears as Irvin picked his brain for information.

"I'm not gonna keep asking you the same questions," said Irvin, standing over the distraught man. "My gun gonna start talking in a minute."

Blackface held his head up in a pleading way. "Them niggas will kill me if I say what I seen."

Irvin cocked the hammer on his revolver. "And I'm gonna kill you if you don't. Make your choice."

It was then that Bradshaw understood what was going on, and there was always more than one way to fuck a cat. He jumped between Irvin and Blackface, talking sense into his head, "Don't shoot the man just 'cause he scared. Blackface is good peoples, and he'll do the right thing under better circumstances."

Frustration did the speaking for Irvin. "I'm tired of being nice to this motherfucker who continue to dance around my questions."

The threat of beef and getting the rest of the package off had been taking a toll on Irvin. From the last numbers quoted, they were seventy-five thousand dollars short of a half-million and still sitting on close to twenty birds. More money could be made with less confusion, but life was a jealous bitch. One step forward always amounted to three steps back. They would never get ahead unless they stayed focused, so Bradshaw kept it leveled. "Just chill and let me talk to him for a minute, okay."

Irvin complied by stepping to the right, gangster-grilling the situation.

Bradshaw scooted a chair close and sat before Blackface, saying, "You watched Ocky, as well as the rest of us, come up in Flag; therefore, you have a moral duty to speak if you know or saw something."

Blackface shook his sweaty, bald head in objection. "Them niggas are dangerous. They'll have my head on the news if I open my mouth."

"Them niggas...who?" Bradshaw took out a big ball of money and plucked a hundred-dollar bill in the man's direction.

Blackface caught the cash note before it hit the floor. Weighing his life on one pan of the scale, his next blast on the other, good judgment escaped along with fear. That dope-fiend mentality kicked right in. "I'm talking about Grub."

Bradshaw watched the sweat dissipate on Blackface's forehead almost instantly, especially after plucking forward the second hundred-dollar bill.

"See, now we're getting somewhere."

"When I was getting a beer, I saw Yancy and Kavy escorting Ocky out the Chinese store with a gun to his side. They put him in a car and disappeared. That was it."

Bradshaw couldn't understand why Yancy and Kavy snatched Ocky after he and Grub had a temporary truce. If the Heights Boys grabbed Ocky for retaliation, that was more logical than what Blackface just disclosed. None of it made sense. "Are you sure it was Yancy and Kavy?"

"Seen the whole thing unfold wit my own two eyes."

Irvin left the room. He could listen to no more because if what Blackface said was true, his friend, Ocky, was probably already dead.

Now that Blackface spilled the beans, diarrhea caught his tongue, "And Butcher been making his presence felt, beating the concrete, asking around about you. He feels like soon as you came home, which isn't a coincidence to most of the hood, bodies started dropping, shootouts left and right. He's out to get you."

Bradshaw didn't know what bothered him the most, Ocky missing or Butcher. Both situations had him frazzled. Neither could be overlooked. At least he knew Butcher's angle, but Ocky was yet to be found. The latter was his greatest concern, not his only worry. He'd done a lot of cheek-turning since touching the bricks, but, even if Ocky was returned dead or alive, Yancy and Kavy had to pay in blood.

Bradshaw thanked Blackface for the info and sent him on his way.

Seconds later, Lisa barged through the door with the whole crew in tow. The woman was screaming to the top of her lungs, "Oh, my God! They just found Ocky with his brains out!"

Something snapped inside Bradshaw when he heard that, flipping on his kill-switch. His mind was convinced Yancy and Kavy had to die. Not tomorrow or the day after, tonight. If he was lucky, both were probably somewhere around the projects or loitering at the barbershop. Bradshaw geared up, taking Irvin and Ed along to waste Grub's two main shooters.

$ $ $ $

Bart circled Spring's residence twice before conjuring the confidence to make his move. Discovering a blind spot at the perimeter of the property, behind a large tree which separated her lawn from a knoll, from that angle Spring was heedlessly placed under surveillance until each light inside her home died. Recovering a crowbar from the bed of his pick-up truck, Bart crept onto the lawn, concentrating his attention on the front entrance, a window and patio door. Unable to gain entry by jamming the lock open,

Bart shattered a sheet of glass, welcoming himself into her lavish dwelling.

Laying everything on the line, even if he had to rape and torture her into submission, Bart was determined to have his way. Her vagina would be his slave.

$ $ $ $

Leaving no rock unturned, the trio thoroughly combed Flag House for their targets but were unsuccessful. They hit the barbershop, still nothing. Far from quitting, it was Irvin's idea to troll Yancy and Kavy's original stomping ground, which was Greenmount Avenue. While cruising up that main artery of the city, two traffic lights after crossing North Avenue, Ed spotted the same blue Caprice he pelted with bullets during that shootout down the projects.

Not even a half block from the Caprice, surrounded by a group of young hustlers, Yancy and Kavy were off to the side of the corner store, engaged in a dice game.

Bradshaw could have spun the bend and hit the two with a drive-by, but that wasn't his style. Up close and personal was always more effective. As the Lexus cut into the alleyway, Irvin was instructed to park, stay behind the wheel and keep the engine hot. "Me and Ed gonna dog these niggas."

Irvin contested, "Yo, Ocky was just as much my boy as anyone elses. I want a piece of them chumps, too."

Bradshaw shared his take, "We can't leave the car unoccupied. I feel more comfortable with you staying behind."

"Why?"

"Because you tech on the wheel. I'm confident you can swerve us out of danger in case shit get thick. I know you ain't no slouch, that you would bust your gun just as fast to prove a point, but murder never been your forte.

Play your part by getting us back to the hood in one piece."

Bradshaw's logic did add up evenly. Concealing a sigh, Irvin conceded. "Y'all do them niggas dirty. Let off an extra shot for me."

"Got'chu. Want for something else." With that, Bradshaw rolled his mask down and hopped out the car.

As a kid of not many words, Ed followed suit, bending one corner, cutting past another. Humidity rose; the distinct scent of death stole the air.

Crouching behind a dumpster, observing the dice game from an alleyway, they patiently waited for the right moment to blast. Soon as Kavy grabbed the bones talking shit, Bradshaw and Ed used that small distraction to their advantage, pouncing down on the group at light speed. Ed was the first to pull his trigger.

[BOOOOOOM!]

That initial shot caught Yancy in the back, releasing a crimson mist. The crowd scattered.

[BOOOOOOO0OOM! BOOOOOOOOM! BOOOOOOOOM!]

Bradshaw's bullets found Kavy's shoulder, neck and head as he attempted to bail. The way Kavy collapsed proved he was an immediate done deal. Yancy clawed at the ground in a slow, agonizing crawl.

[BOOOOOOM! BOOOQOOOM! BOOOOOOM! BOOOOOOM! BOOOOOOM!]

Those five shots came from Ed's weapon, turning the back of Yancy's skull into Swiss cheese.

The two slayings didn't take five seconds. So, with a job well executed, the masked men got low.

It was definitely time for Irvin to get a new whip.

$ $ $ $

Spring awoke to the silhouette of a person standing beside her bed. The horror of coming face-to-face with an intruder seized her. That unknown image moved swiftly, pinning her semi-naked body down before she could yelp.

Bullying the cold crowbar against her windpipe, Bart said, "Thought you'd get away from me. Didn't ya, bitch?"

His voice didn't come as a surprise. Having her oxygen cut short stifled Spring's words, "You...you...you've lost you min...mind. Get th...the...hell...of...mmme."

He grunted, "Shut your lips. It's pitiful bitches like you that make the black race look bad. Committing to one thing, doing another. I gave you enough time to stand on your word, but you spun me. I'm here to collect my just due."

"You're a madman!"

He ripped the sheets off her. "You haven't yet a clue."

Spring toiled to fight him off with every ounce of her being, scratching and kicking. The reason for his presence could not have been more precise: He intended to rape her, but she refused to cower under his assault. Nevertheless, the more she fought, the more it seemed to arouse him. When her panties got torn from her ass, the event that followed got fuzzy.

Now with nothing but air standing between him and her wet hole, Bart yanked out his infant-sized penis and took aim. Once the head made contact with her wetness, the remaining few inches slid in as easy as a pinky finger.

Bart humped away like a horny rabbit. Spring's continued hits landed to no avail. As his heavy testicles smacked her anus with each stoke, his dick was so small the woman wasn't sure if she was even being penetrated.

Allowing him to violate her person, with total immunity, was an emotional trauma she wasn't equipped to live with. Had she known that deceiving him would produce this kind of result, she might have reconsidered before hand. Not having enough time to ruffle through the pro's and con's of her next move, Spring's fingers crawled toward the bronze alarm clock on the nightstand. Being inside of her womb, raw and what he deemed deep, incited his nerve endings, sifting sweat from every pore. Caught in the heat of the moment, Bart bore down at her, losing focus of her hands. It was that mistake that came with a fatal price tag.

In a convoluted state of mind, believing that Bart would probably go as far as trying to murder her after the ordeal, she feared if her own survival was even an option. If she was too inferior or weak to compete and prevail, that was a matter of opinion yet to be proven. But not fighting for her life, Spring imagined the inevitable outcome that Bart would do whatever to cover his tracks. She had one chance to gain traction over the situation, to walk away breathing and she took it. Stocked with a will to live and defiant glow in her eyes, Spring seized the bronze clock and cracked him across the head with the heavy object.

[Cluuuuuk]

It immediately knocked him silly.

[Cluuck! Cliiink! Bing!]

Spring wild him out with the clock until he was unconscious ontop her. She pushed Bart over on his side and came down with the clock against his skull a few more times. Before Spring knew it, her sheets were decorated with nothing but blood and brains. Undergoing a sudden swell of adrenaline, being it her first time killing a man, Spring could not have been more satisfied with her own actions. But as reality slowly crept into view, hysteria faded.

Now looking down at the dead man in her bed took a different image, one that spelled hard prison time if the cops didn't buy her side of the story.

Though she had all the fact's he'd broken into the house and sexually assaulted her, she still wondered what type of heat would be up her ass over such a serious event. That wasn't the attention she needed. If she could dispose of all evidence without a soul knowing, that would better her situation.

So, instead of calling the cops, Spring leaped off the bed, racing to her shed to grab a hacksaw and shovel. She planned to dismember the body and bury it in a place it wouldn't be found.

CHAPTER 11

Even as Ocky's corpse was in the beginning stages of embalming, rather than hit the trash job or join Irvin down the projects, Bradshaw entered Monday morning by attending Jake's wake. The funeral home was practically empty. Either 8:00 a.m. was too early for grieving loved ones or Jake really didn't have many friends. Bradshaw was so numb, yet so infuriated over how his buddy didn't deserve such a bitter consequence, he couldn't cough up a single tear while paying respects. Dusting Yancy and Kavy wasn't enough get-back. They were considered two slimeballs; Jake was a good man. The score was definitely uneven. Grub was up and eventually had to be checkmated, shut down completely.

For that reason among others, Bradshaw skated straight to Grub's downtown office after the viewing. Come to find out, reading the advertising sign out front regarding available office spaces, the fifteen-story building was being leased by no other than Grub himself. Passing some official armed guards at the door, Bradshaw headed to a reception station in the middle of the capacious lobby. Behind the counter was a beautiful, blond-haired, blue-eyed woman.

He greeted her cordially, "Hello. My name is Mr. Peatican. I'm here to see Mr. Mitchells."

She strolled through her schedule log and seen the appointment. However, delighting in her occupation, the receptionist double-checked by calling the Big Man. Following a conversation containing literally five words and a few nods of the head, the visitor was allowed to take an executive elevator directly to Grub's top-floor office.

As the elevator ascended and the sound of light jazz played a calm melody, Bradshaw begun to fathom Grub's influence and power. He thought about how well the fat bastard had his shit together. It appeared he had serious legal enterprises raking crazy dough. Any other dude wouldn't want to jeopardize legit business over street mess, but Grub wasn't like unto any other nigga Bradshaw ever known. He was a greedy individual, selfish, not doing squat for nobody unless obtaining something in return. Pawning the barbershop off was really nothing, but, if he figured Bradshaw could be bought into good graces, he was in for a rude awakening.

When the elevator door opened, Bradshaw stepped into the distinct aroma of a Cuban cigar.

Choked inside of a navy-pinstriped suit, Grub was standing near a bay window that overlooked the whole downtown area. To his left was a mahogany desk stacked with security monitors; to the right was a large hot tub and small putting green. Grub turned to face Bradshaw, "Can you believe your eyes?"

Bradshaw slid in a little joke to throw him off, discouraging any negative energy concerning Yancy and Kavy getting slumped, "Damn, shorty, you done went corporate on a nigga."

Grub sauntered to his desk, explaining, "White folk don't allow colored this far in the game. But when the pussy this good, can't just put the head in."

Bradshaw sat across from him and asked, "Where's that paperwork?"

Fetching the deed to the barbershop, Grub dug into his desk drawer without hesitation. Signing it over in Bradshaw's face, the deed exchanged hands.

Bradshaw scribbled his John Hancock, and the deal was legally sealed.

"Good looking."

Instantly seeming a bit fidgety, Grub lounged in his chair. "That's that. Done. Now you and I need to talk on another level."

Here came the bullshit as usual. "What level is that?"

Grub scoffed, "Stop acting like you're in the blue. Them little bitches made a move on my team last night, kilt two of my hitters. I know you heard about it..."

Bradshaw showed a taste of bewilderment as though the information was new. "Oh, so Kavy and Yancy were your people?"

"Damn right,'" Grub stood on the facts, "two of my best torpedoes."

Bradshaw tried not to reveal his inner-amusement. He was conscious of what he'd done by smashing the two. Their deaths shook Grub's infrastructure, weakening his military. Willie D and Tim-Tim were straight chumps, both better skilled in the business aspect of Grub's empire. Bradshaw viewed neither a threat. "Them 127 Boys were upset about Ocky. The streets said Kavy and Yancy did it. I guess payback is a bitch."

The trajectory of Grub's next statement shot from the belly. "That's absurd! My hitters were ordered to leave that whole situation alone, especially while that Yella shit was going on. My hitters had nothing to do with Ocky. That's my word. That call was made by someone else."

Letting his words go in one ear and out the other, Bradshaw seen Grub as the fat liar he'd always been. Couldn't teach an old dog new tricks. Confident in the scoop he pulled out of Blackface,

Bradshaw uttered, "Yo, I got an eye-witness who saw Kavy and Yancy escorting Ocky from Bells Carryout at gunpoint. What you say to that?"

"It's not possible," spittle flew from Grub's mouth, "I gave them that night off. They would never disobey me. They were loyal—"

"So was Jake."

Guilt made Grub look away.

"Just as I figured," said Bradshaw in a grave tone. "When heads get put to bed, everybody suffer. Rain pour on both sides. No one is exempt."

Almost hyperventilating, Grub left that where it was and said, "I need you to smooth this over for me. While you're still trying to gain specifics about Yella, pick brains, talk to them kids and let them know any perceived beef on my end is dead. It seems they've already merked their supplier, and they don't need a goon like me on their heels. Tell them just like that, what I said word for word. Pump it up a little more if you have to."

That's all Bradshaw wanted to see and hear. If Grub didn't plead for this type of assistance from him, Bradshaw would've thought he had other trusted killers on standby. Besides hiring some hungry mercenaries to do his dirty work, apparently Grub didn't have an extensive military branch beating the streets. Bradshaw belligerently chuckled at having his adversary down bad. "You ah trip."

Agitated, Grub asked, "What the hell is so funny?"

He pocketed the deed. It was bubble-busting time and Bradshaw enjoyed it. "First and foremost, Yella was killed for an entirely different reason that is none of your business. And secondly, that work in the 127 Building is mine."

The cogs in Grub's mind turned as he struggled to register what was just said. "So...so this is all you, your power play the whole time?"

"You should've known I wanted my piece. Part of my muscle made you and the projects. As of this moment, I'm claiming my crown."

Instead of fuming, Grub conducted himself as a businessman. Attempting to salvage the situation, he said, "There's enough cash down Flag for the both of us. With your muscle and my unlimited resources, we could lock down not just the projects but the whole Baltimore. Remember...us family got to stick together."

Bradshaw wasn't with none of that. "Yeah, family, we definitely could."

Grub was about to smile.

"— But we're not. I don't trust you and neither does my crew. It would be of great benefit if you stay out of my way."

The potential smile never reached Grub's cheeks. "What are you referring too...the whole Flag?"

That's not exactly what Bradshaw meant. His sights were just on the 127 Building. But since Grub mentioned it that way, Bradshaw shot his Jumper only to see where it would land. 'Fuckin' right, the whole Flag. I want you out of the 107 and 126 building's as of today. You can either move out by choice or force; that's up to you."

Knowing how Bradshaw once played with that gun, Grub chickened out right before him. To give him the buildings meant he would inherit the beef with Park Heights. "Fine. You can have the projects. That's small potatoes. My money up. You need that hellhole more than me. Consider it an extended welcome-home gift."

It wasn't easy to conclude his demand. "You and I know Flag House always been rightfully mine. And if any of my crew get as much as a scratch on their tennis, I'm personally coming for you."

"Is that a threat?"

Bradshaw stood. "It's a promise."

Grub guffawed, "Is it anything else you're try'na fuck me out of while you're here?"

Bradshaw donned a sarcastic smirk. "Like you said, when the pussy this good, can't just put the head in. I'm done talking."

Grub went mute. Watching in silent rage as Bradshaw entered the elevator, he vehemently slammed his fist onto the desk once the door closed. Grub fumed at how he should have killed Bradshaw before becoming a problem, but he let Tim-Tim talk him out of it.

That's okay. His so-called future brother-in-law currently had the upper hand. Grub had no choice but to wait until Bradshaw slipped. If or when he did, that would be his ass!

$ $ $ $

Euphoric over the unexpected, extraordinary agreement that came about during a simple meeting, Bradshaw rode to the 127 Building feeling like a pure king. It was more than amazing, rather epic how he solidified an impromptu agenda with minor repercussions. Don't get it wrong, Jake and Ocky were missed, but their sacrifice played a precious role in the construction of a greater scheme; therefore, their deaths weren't in vain. That priceless reality truly helped him conquer his grief.

When Bradshaw gathered the crew to share the news, like a four-year- old, even Irvin hopped around in the middle of Lisa's living room. Having the entire hood to their disposal meant triple the money at a faster pace. So the amount of time it would take them to reach their Miami goal had just been cut in half. With Grub pulling out, no competition could stand in their way, so long as the connect kept the work consistent. The crew were on the path of obtaining a success far beyond their wildest dreams.

But success never came without a cost. Bradshaw was informed that the police been off the hook, jumping out on niggas left and right, even blitzing the building on the real-live-gladiator tip. Thank God the crew were always two steps ahead. Bradshaw informed them to stay on point while, evidently, the law were on a mission to set them up. If they haven't seen a customer in the past, the crew were instructed not to serve that person, at least not until shit cooled down. As they dealt with the politics of the day-to-day operation, Bradshaw would work on a blueprint for the 107 and 126 Building's.

Ensuing his visit to the projects, Bradshaw sling-shotted to the parole spot. By way of exception, his case file was called by some rookie parole officer. When inquiring about Ms. Rice, Bradshaw was told she was out sick for the day. That put him on edge. To his knowledge, Spring was devoted to her job, never taking off. And if she was sick, why hadn't she called him? Something wasn't right. Bradshaw went through the normal formality, answering redundant questions, submitting a urine sample before he left. Once outside, he immediately called Spring.

She picked up on the first ring.

Bradshaw heard sniffles. "Baby, you okay?"

She whispered in tears, "I don't know. I'm scared."

"Of what? Of who?" Bradshaw was on full alert. "Where are you?"

Spring paused and then said, "Home."

Bradshaw ordered her to not leave the house. "I'm on my way."

$ $ $ $

In one of many back alleys on Park Heights Avenue, Tyson and Rabbit chopped it up with their mole. No feedback recoiled since their last move. That murder was done on a hunch, on a man's word opposed to concrete information.

Blackface declared, "Dat group of names I gave y'all, like I said before, they may or might not be involved in Yella's death. I don't know for sure. But after y'all smashed Ocky, their big men —"

Tyson interrupted, "What big men?"

Blackface shrunk within his own fear, then said, "Irvin and Bradshaw grilled me about what I saw. I mentioned nothing 'bout y'all, told them those kids, Yancy and Kavy, did it. When two project forces turn on each other, that's how the real truth comes out."

Neither boy was impressed. Bradshaw was a household name; Irvin didn't ring a bell; nevertheless, Tyson and Rabbit heard about the two murders involving Grub's hitters, Yella's little brother wanted to know one thing.

"Why you ain't mention nothing about this Bradshaw and Irvin before?"

That question was a mile beyond his answer. "Because I ain't know until word got back I saw something. I knew about Ocky,

Tabo, Fred, Ed and Sparky. I seen them posted up in the 127 Building, the building where Yella got killed in front of. They pumping turbo crack out of there."

Tyson mugged Blackface. "So you never saw Irvin or Bradshaw chilling around that building?"

Blackface spoke facts until there was nothing left but lies. "Yeah, I have, but they're always on the move. Thought nothing of it."

It didn't sit right with Rabbit that Blackface left out those two relavent names. The boy wasn't sure if the man was blowing smoke up his ass. To get to the marrow, they needed to rap with Grub face-to-face, the man to whom Blackface owed no loyalty.

Assuming a deceitful job well-done on his behalf, Blackface said, "I did what I could for now. If it ain't too much to ask," he smirked and sniffed as though having a pile of heroin under his nostrils, "I'd like another payment before we move on."

His crackhead-greed turned Rabbit's kettle red. The fiend's truth came in scraps, expounded upon in a manner unbefitting to even the eardrums of a pure lame.

Tyson looked at Rabbit. "You heard the man. Go head, pay him."

Awaiting Rabbit's response, Blackface's cheeks tightened with expectancy.

Rabbit paused, returning the stare of a mindless killer, and then whipped out a small caliber weapon.

Blackface stiffened with fright before feeling four bullets pierce his heart like a long-lost love.

$ $ $ $

The second that Detective Butcher received word from his confidential informant, concerning the crackshop being ran out of the 127 Building, he handpicked a special task force. Butcher was working on getting a warrant to storm Lisa's apartment, but without showing probable cause the judge wasn't convinced of any illegal activity at the residence. Therefore, the detective orchestrated a sting operation. His plan was to send an undercover to Lisa's apartment to personally purchase some stones. That form of hand-to-hand would be more than enough to secure a warrant to raid.

Butcher not only anticipated the bust but also hoped to get a crew member to implicate Bradshaw. On a humble, chasing a reliable tip, he caught Bradshaw red-handed with a kilo. But that was the past. Good fortune like that never visited twice. Even rodents learned from their mistakes. Specifically for the sake of tweeking his own strategy to address change, the detective would have to resort to the basics of good, old fashioned police work.

To snag his target this time, Butcher planned on working from the bottom to the top. One thing for certain, if he jammed Bradshaw up once before, he could do it again. No criminal was more clever than the law. Period.

$ $ $ $

Bradshaw made it to Spring faster than he thought humanly possible, the wheels of his whip coming to a skid in front of her property. He hoofed it up her walkway, racing to his woman's aid. The eager guy came in contact with Spring curled up on the patio, her pink pajamas so dirty it appeared brown. Even with the weather claiming a high temperature, obviously in some state of shock, she shivered from head to toe.

Bradshaw snatched her into his arms. "What the hell happened?"

Consistent with the traits of a temporary stupor, Spring babbled a sentence void of vowels.

He hugged her tighter, gently planting kisses on her nose and forehead. "Baby, you're not making any sense. Take your time. I'm here. Nobody's going to hurt you. Whatever happened is over."

She wept for a couple minutes before gluing herself together. After sawing Bart into pieces and earthing his remains in the woods, she drove his truck into a river just a mile from her home.

Even cleaning up the scene came without strain. It wasn't until hearing Bradshaw's voice that she finally broke down. In that moment, Spring grew unsure if what she initially plotted was worth the mental anguish and unforeseen bloodshed. Besides, Spring wondered if she'd done all this planning over a man who refused to come clean and be honest about himself.

When the crying stopped, Bradshaw asked for the umpteenth time, "What happened?"

Refraining from mentioning a word about Bart, Spring slowly snuffed. "I just had an episode, that's all. I'm fine now."

"What type of episode got you like this? I'm confused."

Now was a rare opportunity to capitalize off of his confusion. Lf she couldn't use this to bait him into opening up, likely, he never would. "I fell into an emotional episode because of you. I'm tired of the secrets. I am stumbling over hills for you and it's only right that I learn, know and understand the man I'm falling in love with. You say you're right here, but are you really? If this is true...tell me who's the real person behind that smile."

She wasn't the only one falling in love; he was into her equally.

Bradshaw struggled with trust issues, but Spring had yet to cross or hurt him; therefore, her reaping the torment of those who broke his heart in the past wasn't fair. For all that, she might as well been Peaches. The fact remained a couple couldn't have true love without trust. So, in choosing to love her, he chose to take that chance. Bradshaw would rather be viewed as a thug than a dishonest dude. Hence, he decided to spread the true pages of his life. "Look, I live by a simple code: Honor God, Family...then the Hood. Loyalty is life."

"I'll be loyal," she promised.

He continued, "You already know a lot about where I came from, but I figure you are more concerned about my present and plans for the future."

She nodded in affirmation.

"I'm back in the game, deep. My little crew need me, need me to show them how to survive them streets. I know there's better ways, but this is our way. Right now the streets are going through a big transition. As you know, change brings certain reactions. Unfortunately, sometimes that reaction is violent."

Spring chimed, "Stop beating around the bush. Break it down like I'm one of your niggas."

Bradshaw paused at her statement, squinting momentarily, then added, "Me and Irvin muscling Flag House, just took over all three buildings. Life is about to be beautiful if we stay at it. That's what I been up to."

She stared at him without criticism, expression unreadable.

He became his own judge and jury. "With you being a parole officer, I'm sure you might cut me off after knowing this. I don't want to mess up your perfect life."

"Nobody is perfect," she assured. "We all have skeletons."

Bradshaw was relieved to see her show understanding.

Spring welcomed his dirty laundry. "Are you ready for me to tell you what I've been through and my view of the future?"

Though pleasantly surprised by her initiative, he steeled himself for what he might hear. "Ready as I can be."

With that, bathing in the connection with her lover, Spring gave him a full disclosure of her life. She started from childhood to her parents, from high school to college, from stripping in Miami to juicing men, from identity theft to money laundering.

There's no way Bradshaw could have braced himself for that ten or so minutes of narration. He was blown away. "Damn, I thought I was the one in deep."

"I got everything setup. All I need is muscle to execute," she confirmed.

Bradshaw saw her vision clearly. "And, I guess, that's where you expect me to come in?"

Spring nodded. "That's my plan."

"Why me?"

"Because of your gangster reputation. If you was the face of my operation, dudes wouldn't play with you. We could climb to the top together, as one. You don't have to involve yourself in the drug game. I've made a lot of money through the years. In other words, I'm financially set. You'll be good."

Bradshaw processed the information silently. It sounded like a wonderful opportunity, but he couldn't leave his niggas on stuck. A person like that was a sellout. "I don't mind busting that move with you. Far as my crew, I can't kick them to the curb or sever my ties with the game right now. I need at least two more weeks to keep my head clear of any other responsibility besides what I'm focusing on. I'll then step from the forefront and be able to focus on other things. Hope you understand."

That kind of disappointed Spring, but she had no choice but to play by his rules. Though he was made aware of her plans, she still comprehended the need to handle his personal business before coming on board. "Well, when you solidify your position out in the streets, we can focus on strengthening my...our laundering racket."

"Bet."

A sloppy kiss sealed the deal.

"Oh," Bradshaw broke their lip-lock by going into his pocket, "I got that barbershop."

She examined the deed. "Beautiful. I'm so proud of you. This is a nice step."

He winked. "It's just a start."

"When I get back to the office tomorrow, I'll document this pertinent information into your file."

"Thanks for your support."

Spring had to be extremely careful in making suggestions. Any show of favoritism would throw up a red flag at her job. "With this new source of income, you could trade in your trash gig. Whatever you chose to do on the books, we'll have to execute it quick and be done with it. Keep it clean."

"Wouldn't have it no other way," he concluded. Fact was Bradshaw hadn't thought that far into how to shed his job. Spring was correct in her ideas. He promised to take it into account.

At that point, nothing else was discussed. The focused couple went into the house to wash and fuck. After the hormonal parade, Bradshaw broke away, leaving Spring with a promise he'd return.

$ $ $ $

Once Officer Morgan was disguised and debriefed by his supervisor, Detective Butcher, the undercover patrolman broke camp en route to the 127 Building. The officer was a young father of four sons, each mirroring his bronze complexion and burly build.

He'd be disgraced if one of his boys fell victim to the destructive plight of narcotics. Seller or buyer were the same in his eyes. Both were despicable, having no meaningful place in society. Morgan took pleasure in purging the slums, ridding it of lawbreakers, making ita safer place for children and frightened residents.

As day prepared to give a good-bye kiss, spreading orchard clouds across the sky, fiend's tattered corners like roaches. Clad in a sordid jacket and some dusty cutoff jeans, Morgan did his best to blend in. He actually did a marvelous job infiltrating the junkies, imitating one all the way to the 127 Building. Without drawing a single tip, he shared the elevator with a disruptive group of adolescents, calmly pressing the button to Lisa's floor as if living within the high-rise his whole life.

The door opened as fast as it closed. Bracing himself before exiting the fifth-floor elevator lobby, he took a deep breath and put on a crackhead bop.

Parlaying in front of the designated apartment were two dudes. He approached the fellas, saying, "Hey, I'm trying to score. I hear the lady who lives in this apartment has the best stones in town. I need fifteen dimes. Can y'all help me?"

Immediately realizing something was completely odd about this picture, Irvin and Tabo looked at each other. This was the first time a so- called fiend ever came directly to Lisa's house to cop drugs.

All transactions were conducted on the steps, no place else. It's clear the geeker who posted up before them was either an informant or a stick-up boy.

Irvin responded, "Yo, we have no clue what chu talking 'bout. You must be on the wrong floor."

Morgan smiled, revealing a gold incisor. "I know where I am. This is Lisa's spot, right?"

That statement set Irvin off. "Dawg, I'm telling you one time to step off."

Morgan's smile turned into a partial frown. "Damn, is that how y'all treat customers?"

Tabo chimed, "This clown ain't right. He smells like a pig."

"You working with the police, huh?" asked Irvin, pushing the man back a step.

"Naw," Morgan shook his head, "I get high like everybody else. I hate the police."

Becoming extremely aggressive, Irvin overlooked the answer given. "Yes you are."

"I'm not."

Tabo leapt forward. "He's probably wearing a wire. Lift your shirt."

Irvin pushed him again, demanding, "Do what the fuck he said. Lift the goddamn shirt and empty your pockets."

Feeling his cover was blown and life in danger, resisting the orders given, he went for his service weapon. The piece barely made it out the holster before Irvin and Tabo jumped on him. In a death tussle, in between punches and elbows, the three fought for the gun. Not even a few seconds into the squabble, the joint went off.

[BOOOOM! BOOOOOM! BOOOOOOM! |

$ $ $ $

At that same time...

When Bradshaw got to the garage depot, his coworkers were still out on a trash route. He strolled to Isaiah's office trailer and tapped on the door.

"Come in," said the boss.

Bradshaw entered with a piece of paper in hand.

"Where you been?" asked Isaiah. "You're running on one foot," he put two fingers together, "this close to a week suspension."

Bradshaw responded by dropping the paper on his desk. "I'm officially handing in my resignation."

Eyeballing the sheet, Isaiah went from assertiveness to disappointment. "Oh, you're leaving the family. Are you sure that's something you want to do..."

He spoke proudly, "I just bought a barbershop. It's best I keep my full focus on that."

Isaiah was impressed by the revelation. "Legal ventures where it's at, son. Doing the damn thing, ain't chu?"

"Trying."

Knowing the average small business usually collapse within the first two years, he retorted, "You're always welcomed back if you flop."

Detecting what Bradshaw could only describe as hate, he smirked. "I have no plans of that happening."

"They never do; nevertheless, I wish you the best."

"Thank you."

The men shook hands and parted.

$ $ $ $

Police Dispatcher: "Officer down. I repeat, officer down. All units are to immediately respond to the 127 Building in Flag House Projects."

CHAPTER 12

It was incumbent upon Tim-Tim and Willie D to deliver the latest news like a hot pizza. Hearing about the officer being shot made Grub happy to disassociate himself with the projects, at least for now. However, sitting in a large conference room within his mansion, the fat man was still visibly upset about having gave his leadership the decree to hand both buildings over to Bradshaw. He ranted, "This motherfucker comes home, within no time, and manages to seize a key territory. What the hell do I pay you clowns for!"

Grumbling something to himself before speaking, Willie D replied, "Well...boss —"

"Boss shit!" He stomped his foot down, answering his own question.

"I must pay you niggas big money to fuck ho's, flood watches, style and profile. It's fuck maintaining my enterprise."

Tim-Tim tried to explain —

Grub didn't let him get a word out. "You better not say shit. Clamp your beak. Wasn't you the one who told me we ain't have to hit Bradshaw?

And don't think for one goddamn second I forgot about the promise you made about cooking him yourself."

Tim-Tim struggled to get a lump out of his throat. "I remember, and I'll keep my word."

"Sound stupid," snarled Grub. "You act like you don't know the type of vicious creature he can be when in power. At this point, being that Bradshaw rarely slips, he's probably anticipating a hit coming his way. That window of opportunity has closed."

Knowing that Grub was right, Willie D and Tim-Tim hopelessly hung their heads low.

"Just take a look at yourselves, a fucking pitiful mess. You two disgust me."

Tim-Tim ate the degradation. "So, what do we do now?"

Grub hiked his shoulders like the man had just asked a silly question.

"We pull out and move on."

Willie D spoke, "That's it?"

Grub threw his hand in the air. "For that, yes. But I'm placing an embargo on the whole East Baltimore. They can't cop a rock from me. Let Bradshaw handle that, too. We'll force him to supply that demand along with holding down Flag. He'll spread himself too thin to win. And if he can't feed the hood, which I'm sure he don't have it like that, itll turn on him. The pressure will crush him."

Tim-Tim hung from Grub's nuts. "That's clever."

"I'll also let my shot-callers around the city know not to do any business with him."

Willie D loved the plan as well. "But what if he supplies the demand?"

Grub raised his tone, "Just told you he ain't got it like that, he can't.

The most he holding is three or four joints. Some New York Boy, a dude he might met in jail, blessed him from Uptop."

Tim-Tim weighed that possibility out loud, "Makes perfect sense."

Now lowering his voice to a peg over a whisper, Grub continued to speculate, "When the nigga plugged him in, dude forgot to tell ole Braddy-Brad it wouldn't last. I checked around, even hit a few major lines out of town, nobody sold him squat. They didn't even know he was home. He'll fold, believe me, and I'll eventually pinpoint who he's getting his work from."

"What about Irvin?" Willie D asked.

"He'll get his."

Tim-Tim followed up, "How about Kavy and Yancy? We can't let that ride."

Grub sternly corrected him. "Yes, we can. And we will. I been studying this street life before you got off the porch. Now it's time you set back and learn some shit."

Tim-Tim complied like a scolded child.

With all important topics expounded upon, Grub abruptly concluded their powwow. "Enough gum-jabbing. You two get the hell out."

At the sound of his command, Willie D and Tim-Tim scattered like scared roaches.

$ $ $ $

Bradshaw angrily paced the dinning room of the condo. "How did you let something like that happen? Ah cop...shot in the head. Do you even know how screwed we are!"

With a noticeable tremble of the fingers, Irvin puffed a blunt. "Bro, he didn't identify himself as a cop. He went for a gun and the rest happened. We did what we had to do."

An undercover approaching them meant a hound was onto their scent. All Bradshaw thought about was getting pinched for a conspiracy. "That 127 Building is history. I'm officially shutting it down for good. That coke shop is dead."

Irvin saw pure stress in his mentor's face. "Nobody seen nothing. We good. If you think it's best to permanently close shop in the 127 Building, cool, that's your call, but we still got the other two buildings at our finger tips."

He realized Irvin had tunnel vision. Twenty cops could have gotten shot, that wasn't even enough to convince him to take a chill pill. Bradshaw shook his head in a doomed manner.

"-- Plus, we just made the rest of the money for the connect."

Bradshaw dipped into silence. He was like a zombie.

"Big bro," Irvin tried to get Bradshaw's attention by waving a hand in front of his face, "this situation will blow over. It always do. Cops get shot everyday around the world. Niggas let the heat die and get back to the paper.

We got to keep pushing and stay focused. Those were your words."

Bradshaw remained standing, resting the back of his head against the wall. He took deep breaths, allowing each to expel slowly. He repeated that action until a sense of calm washed over him. Then the mental fog began to clear up. He snapped back into reality and said, "All these constant setbacks have a way of taking a toll. You're on point; this will blow over as with everything else. We just got to concentrate on our next chapter."

Irvin flashed a smirk. "Which is getting this bread to the connect."

Bradshaw gritted his teeth in secrecy. "Right."

Irvin paused, eyes batting to the ceiling and then back onto Bradshaw.

"I got Vanessa to tell Miami about you. And according to her, they are anxious to meet you."

"What?" His statement threw Bradshaw completely off. "Why would you do that when you have yet to meet them yourself?"

"Because you politic better than me. I figured, maybe, you could finesse a better deal."

The moment Bradshaw traveled to Miami alone, that meant Irvin would no longer be the sole pipeline to the connect. He himself would be the top dog. Bradshaw wasn't sure if he was ready for all of that. "I don't know, yo. That's a big move."

A sincere smile conquered Irvin's cheeks. "One that I'm sure you could pull off. Besides, with all this bullshit going on, a small vacation wouldn't hurt none."

His little partner definitely hit the nail on the head. A different scenery, blessing himself with a moment to play the game on offense rather than defense, would suit him well. He needed the fresh air. He conceded, "I'll do it, but next time inform me before you volunteer my services."

Happiness birthed Irvin's kiddy response, "I'll try."

Bradshaw attempted to think three moves ahead. "Though we still got our own bricks to get off, I don't want any type of drug activity going on while I'm away. Pay the crew and give them all a thousand dollar bonus, a little something to hold them over until I get back."

Irvin gave himself a personal job. "Cool. And I'll deal with the streets, scout, organize."

Bradshaw considered questioning on why he lied about that copping from Grub situation, but he withdrew, affording his pupil the opportunity to redeem himself. "You sure?"

"Fuck yeah. Don't worry. I learned from the best."

Bradshaw left it at that. "Make me proud."

"First thing smoking...I'm getting rid of the Lexus."

A brisk simper finally manifested. "You read my mind."

"Like a book."

"Say no more. Let's get back to the business."

The two shared a bro hug and headed to the safe to recount the connects paper.

$ $ $ $

The injured officer was rushed into emergency surgery. Out of the few shots fired, one bullet went through an ear, nonfatally penetrating his brain. Though the shooting left him in a comma, doctors were unsure if he'd make a full recovery. Learning to walk and talk again wouldn't be an immediate process. Tossing a Frisbee, catching a football or getting back to duty were now counted among past-life activities. If and when the officer was blessed to regain consciousness, he would be subject to a new existence, one seized by regret and a bedpan.

It would have taken Butcher three thousand words to confess the depths of his own sorrow. He was committed to finding justice for Morgan as he was obsessed with putting Bradshaw back in shackles and chains. The projects was on lock while Butcher cross-referenced leads that resulted in deadends. While plotting behind the wheel of a cruiser, his main focus was on Bradshaw and the five names targeted as crew members. Above the obvious, an informant mentioned his subject being romantically involved with Spring Rice. Butcher did his homework and discovered Ms. Rice was Bradshaw's Parole and Probation Agent. Perhaps, that was the leverage the detective needed. He decided it worthwhile to pay her a visit.

$ $ $ $

Since that police got smashed, the drug business was extremely dry down Flag House. Irvin saw Bradshaw off and slid down the projects to check the heat level, finding two more reliable stash houses in the 107 and 126 Building's. He planned to have the groundwork of operations up and ready by the time Bradshaw got back in town. That would show his big homie two minds were better than one. While walking through the basketball court behind the 107 Building, Irvin ran smack into Grub and his two fuck boys.

The air got instantly thick.

The fat man was the first to block his path. "What up, little bitch ass nigga? So you rolling with Brad, huh?"

Traveling naked, regretting the fact of leaving his gun in the car, Irvin stayed calm. He answered pridefully, "No doubt."

With Tim-Tim and Willie D posted by his side, Grub shouted, "How the fuck you gonna bite the hand that fed you for the last few years!"

Chest out, feet planted on a forty-five degree angle, Irvin blatantly dismissed him. "Yo, this business, nothing personal. I don't owe you shit."

Seeing the boy refused to be intimidated, Grub curved... "I guess it's about time you got some heart, but just know that this little operation yall got won't last. When Bradshaw go back to jail, y'all will come crawling back to me. With or without these buildings, I still run Flag House Projects, always will."

Irvin read him with his eyes. "Let cha mouth tell it, but we both know you don't run shit down here no more. This Bradshaw trap."

Tim-Tim exposed the butt of a revolver in his waistline.

Irvin tensed up but tried not to show it. "If you gonna shoot me, shoot. Make sure you kill me. But understand when Bradshaw finds out, he won't miss."

Grub signaled Tim-Tim to put his shirt back down.

Once Irvin seen they were bluffing, he dragged on them. "Y'all three are some stone-cold coons. And the next time you flash a gun on me, you better use it."

Grub endeavored to check him. "Don't get big headed."

"Man, fuck y'all," responded Irvin, barging straight through the middle of the three.

"Our boss ain't finish talking to you," yelled Willie D.

"Kill yourself!" Screamed Irvin in the wind.

His bold actions left them speechless. They paused and watched him cut the corner.

$ $ $ $

Miami, Florida

When Bradshaw stepped out the terminal at Miami's International Airport, he went straight to baggage claim. A sigh of relief was experienced when his hands and the suitcase reunited, for it contained the money owed to the plug. The Blazing sun nursed on his melanin the moment he emerged from the doors of the Airport.

231

Armed with just a phone number, Bradshaw was stunned to see an eggshell-white limo waiting at the curb. The driver jumped out, prompted him for his luggage, and placed the suitcase in the trunk. Irvin urged him to wear a purple shirt and cap, and Bradshaw figured the color scheme was how they identified him.

An older fellow in an Italian suit descended a tinted window, using a head gesture to motion him inside. The man looked of Cuban decent. His tan skin was glossy, unspoiled by wrinkles or blemishes. Bradshaw took in rich fumes of imported cologne once sitting across from him. He looked like a boss, even smelled like one.

Bradshaw was first to comment, "It's a pleasure to meet you."

The guy smiled, responding cordially, "Welcome to Miami. Are you a virgin to this city?"

He'd been there before, but the short tour wasn't worth mentioning. "Yeah, but I'm not a regular."

The man visually studied him without breaking a stare, patting him down for a hidden weapon. Once verifying the visitor was clean, he tapped his shoulder with a smile.

In the face of the connect, Bradshaw could only wonder what he was thinking. "Where are we headed?"

A response came in the man's Latin accent, "To an estate in Coral Gables."

He heard about that section of Miami. It was reserved for the extremely wealthy. "Sounds like a plan."

The Cuban rejected further conversation, drawing his face to one side. "Speak less and enjoy the sights."

Bradshaw nodded and sealed his lips.

Just off the ocean, the estate sat upon sixty acres. Traveling up a hill as far as the eye could see, the Macedonian Mansion was reposed at the center of the well fortified property. Armed guards in black slacks held sentry at the entrance. Some roamed on foot, others patrolled on customized buggies, but all were armed with assault riffles. Bradshaw noticed a helicopter ontop a roof. A golf course was next to a dock with a large yacht anchored. The property was a true example of success. The limo came to a halt in front of the mansion. When Bradshaw vacated the luxurious ride, double doors swung open and there stood a minor no more than the age of ten or eleven.

She was clad in a maroon jumpsuit with gold lion heads for buckles. Maybe an inch taller than Doobie, chocolate locks stopped at shoulder's length. A smooth brown hue displayed her flesh as silk canvas rather than actual skin. The girl's face was pretty as any heavenly cherub awaiting a lost soul at the crossroads. Standing shoeless made it easy to acknowledge her toenails painted with real sterling silver. A man in casual attire was posted alongside her, in his hands was a black doll baby. Being the one to deliver the first shipment, he leaned down to whisper something in her ear.

The man who accompanied him inside the limo, retrieved the luggage, and rushed to kneel before her, kissing the foot of her plastic doll baby.

Bradshaw didn't really know what to make of the spectacle. One thing was for certain, the fellow who picked him up wasn't the connect at all. Maybe the connect was the man standing beside the child. Based upon his debilitated demeanor, him being any type of authority was unlikely. The doll seemed to be in a more influential position than he.

The little girl sneered in a voice fit for a child half her age, "You're not Irvin."

He heard the safety click off rifles from every angle. "Hold up," he lifted his hands, "I'm Irvin's mentor, more like his big brother. My name is Bradshaw. He sent me in place of himself."

One guard forced him to the double doors, using only the cruel stock of his rifle. Bradshaw was knocked down upon his knees. He and the child were now the same height.

She looked him square in the eye and pointed to the foot of her baby doll. "Kiss it."

Knowing a weapon could take aim at any moment, Bradshaw pecked the doll without hesitation, which became the weirdest thing he'd ever done.

Respected as a killer back home, he was no match against countless guns pointed at him. Satisfied with him meeting the requirements of her ritual, a mellifluous echo tinkled behind a soft voice, "Why did he send you?"

Bradshaw didn't understand why this kid was asking the big questions. "Because I taught him all he knows. We made this money together for the connect. Me, him and Vanessa share the same condo. She and I are like family. You can call and ask her."

With that said, the girl instructed the guard to help Bradshaw to his feet. She gave off a contagious smile, but showing her teeth was just as risky as a frown. Though angelically adorable, a snap of the finger or a flutter of an eyelash could instantly mean the difference between life and death. "Welcome to my playhouse. Come, let's get out of this heat."

Bradshaw was finally able to exhale. A slew of random thoughts gathered into a single picture. Deceived by the first guy in the limo, or should it be said by his own misjudgment, he humbly inquired, "Where is the person I've come to see?"

The girl confirmed, "I am she, Bellamy."

Bradshaw once thought he saw it all, every nook and cranny of the game, until now. Nothing could have prepared him for such a wild voyage. A little girl was actually the plug, the big dog calling the shots. He couldn't believe it. What part of the game is that? That was the only question he continued to ask himself. The Cuban guy handed Bradshaw the luggage as he followed Bellamy into the mansion.

She looked at the suitcase. "Is that what I think it is?"

He remembered the important lives lost in the process of obtaining the bill money. So many personal emotions were attached to that particular bundle of cash. "Yeah, the whole thing."

Her eyes glittered.

Three guards shadowed the two as they entered a spacious playroom.

Few toys were scattered around the marble floor, Thousands of vintage, porcelain dolls hung by their necks from the ceiling. Most were antiques, many dating back to early as the seventeenth century. A desk formed of a rare metamorphic rock, long as a dining table made to accommodate twelve, was stationed near a world map that took up the entire wall. Embedded in the wall, opposite from the desk, was an enormous aquarium. Swimming within its waters were several tiger sharks. At the back wall stood a book shelf with a sliding ladder. In the middle of the room, directly beneath a retractable sunroof, lived an altar-like marble stone. Atop that stone was a large-brass bowl.

Bellamy climbed upon the desk and invited her visitor to the seat nearest to where she stood. He obeyed without incident, handing her the suitcase that contained five hundred thousand dollars. One guard retrieved an automatic money machine, placing it at her shiny toes.

After counting the dough, she took half and dumped it into the bowl ontop of the altar. Time paused as she sung a barely audible lullaby over the cash and struck a match. The money went up in flames. A devious chuckle traveled through her silently.

Bradshaw's brain came to a red light. Toiling to understand the reason behind what he'd just witnessed, realizing the child's insanity was no chore.

When the ritual was complete, Bellamy faced him and_ said, "Money...the root to evil. I split half with the Devil. He's my partner."

He took an intent look at the girl to depict if she was bullshitting, but Bellamy's expression was solid as a tombstone. Before freaking out, he asked, "Now that your dues are paid, can we get down to business?"

She liked how he remained focused on the real issue at hand. "Why am I just meeting you?"

Bradshaw had a shirt older than this little girl. He'd been breaking law before she was even a thought in her daddy's balls, but that was kept to himself. "Because I'm just coming home from prison. You know, the place where adults go for doing bad things."

Feeling that he underestimated her wisdom, Bellamy put a finger to his lips. "Don't insult me. I am far beyond my years. Could a foolish child build the likes of this powerful empire? I've been taught by the best."

Bradshaw held his breath until she was ready to move her hand. He then responded, "I apologize. I was only trying to draw the picture of a place I'm sure you've never been?"

The mention of drawing made Bellamy yearn for crayons, but she declined, keeping her thoughts on a serious note. "I don't like to do business with people I don't know, but I trust Vanessa and her heart's choice, Irvin.

He's a good guy. And since you taught him everything he knows, it is fair to say you're responsible for the success of this first shipment."

Bradshaw's inner flame fell upon darkness. He corrected her, speaking cautiously, "Not me alone, some good dudes died to help us move forward. I was there to point the way."

Bellamy sat behind the desk like a business woman, sinking into the chair to only where her eyeballs were visible. A guard rushed her a pillow, propping her up in a comfortable way.

Bradshaw held back his laughter. Something was odd about this whole arrangement. It definitely wasn't about the bread, not after the stunt she performed. It was time to pick her brain. He made a rational inquiry, "Why am I really here?"

Bellamy gobbled down a small piece of candy before saying, "I have business in your care, so meeting with you is mandatory."

That made sense.

She continued, "There's a lot of product to be moved, and I would like to expand into the Mid-Atlantic region. At the moment, one by the name of Calvin Mitchell has control over that part of the compass."

Bradshaw didn't know exactly how powerful Grub was until now. The plug even knew his name. It was no need to mention their past, present feud nor family ties. To expound on those facts could be more detrimental, at the moment, than actually helpful. Bradshaw listened on.

"He gets his product from the Dominicans in Philadelphia, who happen to be my chief rivals on the entire East Coast. From Virginia on down to the Mississippi River is my territory. I control the drug trade in that area. My rivals control everything above the Mason-Dixon Line."

Maryland was the state that separated the South from the North. The kid was a wizard, practically more intelligent than any child he'd ever seen. She'd race circles around his beloved son. "So you need me to take over my area for you? That way you can tip some power from your Dominican rivals."

She wore a smile, this one not as transmissible. "Only if you are capable as Vanessa says you are."

That statement made him ask, "You knew who I was from the moment I stepped out of that limo..."

She fiddled with a cigar but didn't light it. "Of course, I know everything."

To respond in that way exposed her immaturity. Knowledge was infinite, an ever evolving concept. So to have it was to lose it because it never stopped growing. He shook his head at her child's play. "If I do this for you, what's in it for me and my crew?"

A calculator would have served her well at that point, but Bellamy put the house on him. "An unlimited supply of cocaine. I can provide you kilo's for as little as five thousand each."

Bradshaw didn't trust his own ears. Kilo's for nearly pennies...he could only imagine the boss status of who was supplying her. There had to be a bigger catch. He didn't know whether or not to take the deal.

Bellamy tossed aside the yucky cigar. "It's your right to be skeptical. I won't promise what I can't deliver. You happen to be in the right position at the right time. The rest is up to you."

It couldn't have been said any plainer. Images of the future came to him in smoke, fire and blood. Bradshaw felt he was about to sale his soul to the Devil, but the deal was too good to let slide. "Okay, spit the facts."

Clearly pleased, the glow in her eyes turned to sapphire. Bellamy explained, "I will cosign two hundred kilo's every month. You will pay me one million dollars, but I want that region under my control within a year. From there, we will expand. Sophisticated intelligence and weapons will be at your disposal. Can you dig it?"

She had to learn those end words off of some movie. It was cute. "You got yourself a deal."

Instead of a manly shake, Bellamy extended her hand, palm down, to have her knuckles kissed. After he obliged in that manner, she said, "Now I must get to know you. We'll go out and have some lasting fun."

He busted her bubble, "Baby girl, I can't. I'm on parole back in Maryland. I'm not even supposed to be out of state. My flight is scheduled for 8:30 tonight. I'll soon have to get back to the airport."

A brow sagged, the other trembled, barely maintaining its arch. Out came the fat bottom lip. "But I can put you on a private jet, have it fly you to your condo, and drop you in the living room...if you'd like? You'll beat the sun before it hits Baltimore."

He couldn't resist. "Okay, let's go."

"Yaaaaay!" was her response.

$ $ $ $

Assuming he would accept her offer, Bellamy already leased the whole Walt Disney World for one day. She, her security, Bradshaw and park personnel were the only ones allowed inside. That showed just a small taste of her influence. They partied from the Cinderella's Castle all the way to the Magic Kingdom, missing little in between. While sailing on a jungle cruise in Adventure Island, Bellamy said, "Every one I know is someone...doctors, lawyers, prosecutors, judges, politicians and more. They're all eager to be my friend. Would you like to know why?"

His eyes were following an animatronic ape when he replied, "Sure. Thrill me."

"Because I hold the power to ruin their lives."

Bradshaw's eyes were now on her. "What's that supposed to mean?"

"I made it my business to gather dirt on everyone who's in a position to hurt me."

He wondered who would want to hurt a girl not even old enough to obtain a driver's license. *What kind of enemies did she really have?*

"If I hurt, they hurt."

There was much more for Bradshaw to know, but the time was too soon. He cut to the chase, "You're telling me this to say what?"

Bellamy made sure he heard every word when she reported, "I have ordered more men killed then AIDS and cancer combined. If you mess up a shipment or cross me, you will meet my partner."

It was nothing he could say but, "I respect that, but I got this."

That was the reassurance that sealed the deal.

They continued to party, eating and boarding rides. Bellamy eventually got so exhausted that she fell asleep in his arms. When they got back to the mansion, he handed the child over to her doll carrier. She felt like the daughter he never had. By 3:30 a.m., as promised, Bradshaw flew through the clouds on a private jet. He was now thoroughly in a position to take over the streets. It was a good thing Grub tucked his tail from the projects. For the deal just made, Bradshaw would not only need Flag House but the rest of the city as well.

To Be Continued...

Printed in the United States
by Baker & Taylor Publisher Services